ORC'S CAPTIVE

MONSTER MATE HUNT, BOOK 4

AVA ROSS

ENCHANTED STAR PRESS

ALSO BY AVA ROSS

Mail-Order Brides of Crakair

Brides of Driegon

Fated Mates of the Ferlaern Warriors

Fated Mates of the Xilan Warriors

Holiday with a Cu'zod Warrior

Galaxy Games

Alien Warrior Abandoned

Beastly Alien Boss

Bride of the Fae

A Sci-Fi Holiday Tail

Monsterville, USA

Monster on Board

(co-written with Alana Khan)

Love at First Orc

Monster Mate Hunt

Sweet Monster Treats

Brides of the Zuldrux Warriors

Monsters, PI

Single Titles

A Monster Worth Fighting For

Craving Stardust

Dad Bod Dragon

Mated to the Dragon

Jasmine's Grumpy Genie

Swamp Thing (You Make My Heart Sing)

You can find her books on Amazon.

ORC'S CAPTIVE

Can a wounded orc hero protect his treasured mate from a cruel captor?

Nia: I spend my days healing those forced to battle in my stepbrother's arena and my nights hiding. I've resigned myself to the fact that with my burn scars, I'll never find love. Until my stepbrother commands me to heal his latest acquisition—an orc who was severely injured during capture. I've only heard of orcs, but I do my best to heal him and prepare him for the battles he'll soon face.

As I care for Dakur's wounds, we exchange glances that slowly grow heated. It's not long before I'm falling in love for this gruff, stoic warrior who's as trapped here as me.

Can we find a way free to finally be together?

Dakur: I barely remember being captured, and I've suffered since, forced to fight in a ring while humans bet on the outcome. The only good thing in my life is Nia, the human woman who sparked my clan's pendant. She's my fated mate, though I doubt I'll live long enough to be with her. But as we fall deeper in love, I know I must find a way.

I'm going to get us out of this trap, and then I'm claiming Nia as mine.

Orc's Captive is Book 4 in the Monster Mate Hunt Series. Expect a seductive orc hero with a creative. . . (cough), size difference, a fierce, scarred woman who will do anything to protect those she loves, plus a fantasy world you'll want to live in. HEA guaranteed. Each book is standalone, but the series is more fun if read in order.

Trigger: Nia lives in a dark world, as do the creatures she heals—those her stepbrother forces to fight in the arena. There is no animal death on the page, however. Her stepbrother is mean. He pushes and threatens her.

Monster Mate Hunt
Books in Order:
Orc's Mate
(a prequel novel –
FREE with newsletter sign-up)

Orc's Craving
Orc's Fate
Orc's Maiden
Orc's Captive
Orc's Taming

FOREWORD

Monster Mate Hunt Terms, Characters, General Information

Orc's Mate (takes place 5 years before Orc's Craving):

Zephyr Clan: Air. Pendant is a circular disc made up of swirls to represent the air and water

Characters: Odik Brunellon, Eleri. Their children: Zur, Yusta

Birgid: woman who taunts Eleri and murdered Zur, the hunter who raised Eleri

Cassatine: orc midwife

Crikin: Dakur's father

Drabass: male from Odik's clan

Madine: elderly orc female; the keeper of clan stories

Trilden: Odik's friend

Zarran: Odik's vox

Zur: elderly man who adopted Eleri. They name their son after him

Orc's Craving, Book 1

Azuris Clan: Water/Sea. Pendant: metal swirls with spikes resembling waves

Characters: Rhoslyn, Jaus Kreedaull, Shirra: their daughter

Arkest: oldest, most revered healer

Eamon: village mayor who wants Rhoslyn for himself

Feyla: Jaus's female vox

Kael: older guardsman

King Surled: Jaus & Madr's father

Liall: older orc who runs an herb shop in the orc city

Lyneth: Rhoslyn's sister; married to Sveth

Mastivule: head of the kingdom's guards

Viskeete: rather crude orc

Orc's Fate, Book 2

Lumen Clan: sun/mountains. Pendant: shaped like the sun, it represents the mountains and the heavens above

Characters: Madr Thourand, Lyneth

Brakkis: Madr's vox

Finsteg: Matis Clan male who challenges Madr

Grock: Azuris clan male who guards Lyneth and is murdered

Kael: older village guardsman, friend to Lyneth

Milllamay: shayde Dakur raised

Pulost: Matis Clan male who challenges Madr

Riank: Madr's cousin who wishes to rule

Sessavia: Matis Clan female, welcomes Lyneth

Taen: shayde Dakur raised

Tenkaril: Madr's mother, adopted Zickar; wise woman who "sees" when she touches someone

Tescall: Riank's younger brother and ally

Orc's Maiden, Book 3

Matis Clan: forest. Pendant: spikes from the sun like sunlight stabbing through the canopy

Characters: Zickar, Alwen, their son: Ferrin

Bredar: Alwen's brother

Brillie: Flazant female

Creea: Alwen's sister

Dillu: Flazant male

Loobek: orc male who went looking for Dakur

Mavileen: human woman, leader of the village on the edge of the forest

Nayleen: Alwen's sister

Noul: one of three shaydes Dakur raised

Pirrah: Flazant elder

Roolina: Alwen's mother

Rusket: older orc male

Trillie: Flazant female

Ulong: orc metal worker

Villadeer: Flazant female

Wambak: Flazant male

Orc's Captive, Book 4

Matis Clan

Characters: Dakur, Nia

Brunt: Nia's stepbrother

Kengart: head of Brunt's guards

Lianire: Brunt's second in command

Veegar: human male, cook

Woobedon: Nia's village built in the middle of the vast desert, near an oasis

Orc's Taming, Book 5

Ember Clan: desert/fire. Pendant: flames shooting toward the sky

Characters: Turren, Kaila

Airest: Turren's vox

Brunnen: Kaila's younger brother

Daskin: Turren's second in command

Ferella: female orc, Ember Clan

Gromget: orc game that's a mix of soccer and American football

Jabon: Kaila's boss in the village

Nuark: teenage orc living in the Ember Clan

Reven: teenage orc living in the Matis Clan

Sianna: orcling infant

Urlain: elder in the Ember Clan

Varalar: female smithy at the village

Vox history: Winged creatures fostered in the Ember Clan and bonded with orcs. They form within a seed and when they slip out, they bond with the person closest to them. In earlier days, this was their parent, but now all eligible males and females travel to the Ember clan to be there for the hatching. The bonded orc remains with the hatchling long enough for the vox to grow for flight, feeding and grooming it so it knows their touch and smell. They nest near their bonded orc but return to the Ember territory every three years when they're ready to produce young.

General Terms:

Ashenclaw: creature like a wolf

Aspest berries: found on Odik's island, can be added to tea

Avestilar: large birds who nest high in the canopy

Boolong: creature like a wild cow

Brugel: meat like bacon

Caedos: leader of a clan

Chall: like a cat; kits are their young

Cheerish: type of bird

Clik: distance; about a mile

Daphoon: a dolphin-like sea creature

Doonet: a light cloth made from a plant

Dresalod: vicious, enormous crab-like sea creatures that attack the orc city

Elkern: timid creature like a deer

Effervast trees: fragrant

Emerest stone: rare, found in caverns, Turren compares the color to Kaira's eyes when she's angry

Fillawate: drink made from a rare fruit that grows deep beneath the ground. When fermented and drank, makes someone feel happy, though it's not alcohol

Flazant: stone people born of the boulders around us. Prior allies to the orcs

Hilardep: enormous, venomous spider found in the forest

Lamest: forest snake

Liladek flowers: lovely scent, bloom at night

Lindenmint: herb Rhoslyn drinks as tea; has antibacterial properties, slows a cut's blood flow. Found to be highly toxic to dresalods

Mellabar: a fruit jam

Orcling: orc baby/child

Reskit: creature like a rabbit

Ribber: creature like a rat

Secondist: Tuesday

Shayde: large, vicious, lizard-like creatures who live and hunt in the forest

Sinderfluff: material like silk

Squitt: creature like a squirrel

Succire: a sweet red berry

Tartledge Sea: vast, purple sea beyond the Orc Kingdom

Teegar: plants used to propel orcs to canopy platforms or take them below ground. Serve as elevators. Fed with diluted fillawate.

Teetser: a fly/mosquito

Trulist: trees that grow in thick groves

Wanderer: orc who travels, learning new ways to use their pendants

Weelen leaves: used in tea

Whisp: an insect that, when blown across, lights up. Used in lanterns as a source of light.

Willadon: a black root, made into a tea that relieves arthritis pain

CHAPTER 1
NIA

They called me a monster, but I preferred to think of myself as a mouse. I was tiny, pretty much defenseless, and I could barely resist bolting when anyone came near. Could I be blamed for the latter? If I didn't move fast enough, I'd feel the impact of a fist or the gouge of a blade.

As I hurried down the hillside outside my village after collecting herbs, I rubbed the network of scars on my neck and the right side of my face. I'd long since healed—on the outside. I wasn't sure I'd ever feel healed where it counted most—on my soul. When I looked in the mirror . . . Was it any wonder the villagers called me a monster?

Honestly, the true monster was my stepbrother.

Slinking through the back door of the compound I'd called home since my mother and stepfather died, I paused in the shadows and listened, hearing nothing but the thump of my heart. My breaths were uneven, but that was the norm. Until I'd locked my bedroom door and collapsed on my tiny bed, my breathing would remain erratic.

Keeping my footsteps light, I slunk through the dark hallways with only the soft glow of a whisp lantern to light my way until I came to the door leading to the network of underground passages.

Creatures fought and died down there. So did people.

And this was where those I cared for saw past my exterior to the kind heart I kept hidden from everyone else.

I tiptoed down the wooden stairs, my footsteps echoing around me, only punctuated by a groan or sigh of pain from an injured being. It hurt to think of their wounds and the slashes on their hides.

But I did what I could to heal them.

After slipping past the room where the guards sat playing cards, I moved down the long, narrow hall with walled cages on each side. I stopped at the first and stepped inside, blankly taking in the stone walls, the dirt floor, and the bins containing food and water for the beast. Each was as trapped inside their cage as I was in the compound.

The beast's breaths rose and fell as he lay with his head on the ground and his eyes closed.

When I stepped forward with my basket of herbs and healing supplies hooked on my arm, his head snapped up, and his feral, black-glowing gaze met mine. He scrambled to his four hooves, grunting when his back right leg wouldn't support him.

His low growl rang out.

"It's me, precious one," I whispered, stepping toward him with my hand stretched out.

He sniffed it, and his body relaxed.

"I've come again to help," I said softly, lowering my basket to the floor.

He nudged my hand playfully before settling on the dirt floor once more, his wounded leg extended out beside him. This wasn't the first time I'd helped him, and it wouldn't be the last, or I hoped it wouldn't be the last time, because the alternative was a horrifying death in the arena.

One day, I'd make sure these poor souls were free— and myself, if I could make such a thing happen.

Other than escaping, there was no way out of this trap for either of us.

I made quick work of cleansing his wound, then covering it with a poultice I made from the herbs I'd collected. My only training came from my grandmother, and sometimes, it was all I could do to remember what she taught me before she died when I was ten.

Not long after that, my mother married my stepfather, and I "gained" an older stepbrother, Brunt.

When my mom and stepfather died in the fire, Brunt took over his dad's businesses and the arena. The compound had been here for a very long time. It was built when the village was initially settled, but I didn't know much more about its history than that.

After wrapping a bandage around the beast's leg, I

went to his head and gently stroked his furry cheeks, staring into his soft dark eyes.

"I'm sorry I couldn't find any pain-relieving herbs," I said with an ache in my chest. "But I hope your laceration soon feels better. The poultice will help."

He nudged my belly with his snout and huffed out a breath.

My eyes stung. If only I could do more for him.

After making sure he had enough water and food, I moved on to the next cage. It took hours, but by the time the sun was setting, I'd finished helping all I could and returned to my room.

I couldn't do much else for them, but I hoped what I did gave them a brief moment of comfort.

Until night fell and they were forced into the ring once more.

Inside my room, I washed my hands in the basin.

While I didn't often dare, tonight, I stared at my image in the small mirror mounted on the wall above the wash cupboard, taking in my pale, almost white hair, my light blue eyes, and the network of scars puckering across the right side of my face and neck. The bands of distorted pink flesh stopped below the top of my blouse. I'd survived the fire when my mom and stepfather hadn't, and for that, I was grateful. Better to be scarred than dead.

After dressing in a clean skirt and blouse, I left my room and moved silently through the hall to the kitchen.

"There you are," Veegar said with a wry smile, looking back from where he stood at the stove preparing the meal for Brunt's men. I'd help him with this task and then serve what we made on big platters in the adjacent dining room. Veegar tilted his head to the plate sitting on the counter. "That's for you. Eat it before you do anything else."

My eyes watered once more. "You didn't have to do that. Bread and cheese, plus maybe an apple, would be enough."

"You deserve to eat as well as the others," he said softly, adding more meat and roasted vegetables to my plate. The spicy scent made my belly rumble, reminding me I hadn't eaten since dawn. "Take it to your room if that makes you feel better. I've got almost everything ready for the main meal. I'll collect your plate later."

"I'll bring it back." I hurried over to grab it and an eating implement.

His dark face beamed as he smiled down at me, revealing his fangs. There was a time when this male had taken his place among my stepbrother's warriors, but he'd aged and, thankfully, was assigned to the kitchen rather than tossed out onto the street. A wise move since Veegar was not just a strong warrior, but he was also an amazing cook.

Inside my room, I sat on my bed and ate, savoring the rich spices and subtle flavors Veegar gave each dish. He was wasted on Brunt and his crew. He should be running a restaurant in a big city. Although, the only city I knew of was many weeks of walking from here. Our village had been built near an oasis in the middle of an enormous desert, and other than a few migrating orcs who kept their distance as they passed outside the village limits, I'd seen no one but the descendants of families whose relatives settled here ages ago.

Finished, I'd set my empty plate on the low table beside my bed and was sliding off to take it back to the kitchen when someone banged on my door.

The knob rattled.

My heart leaped into my throat, making it a challenge to swallow. "Yes?" I squeaked.

"Get down to the beast area," my stepbrother barked. "Now."

"I've already cared for everyone."

"Not this one."

Ah. So he'd brought a new one in, had he?

One of these days, a beast would go feral and kill him. While I knew it was wrong of me, I looked forward to seeing him lying still on the dirt floor, maybe within one of the cages, while one of his "fighters" ripped him apart. He deserved it after what he did to them.

"I'll go," I said in a high-pitched voice. If I didn't quickly agree, he'd break down the door and make sure I understood the importance of following through on his commands.

"Now." With that, his footsteps moved away.

I gathered my things and, with the plate in my hand, scurried to my door, unlocking it to peek out. Spying no one in the hall, I hurried to the kitchen, though Veegar wasn't there. I could hear him in the dining room, serving the men and my stepbrother. Boisterous calls for more ale and food echoed in the adjacent room.

If I was lucky, I could take care of the wounded animal and get back to my room before they drank too much ale. My stepbrother wasn't good about protecting me from his men when he'd had too much to drink. Without alcohol, the only one he didn't protect me from was himself.

With my basket hanging over my arm, I sped down the steep stone stairs, the coldness sliding off the walls, sinking into my bones and rattling them. At the bottom, I paused and composed my face into a mask of indifference. It never paid to show that I felt affection for those I healed.

"Come to see the new one, have you?" The head guard, Kengart, asked, his gaze traveling down my frame, though without a sneer. One corner of his lips twisted up, making the knife scar spanning his face from his left temple to the skin below his right ear twist.

"Yes." I kept most of my attention on his feet. Eye contact was often seen as an invitation to touch. While Kengart left me alone, and my stepbrother's men had a healthy respect for his fist, they weren't above a grope here and there.

"I'll come with you," he said.

I shrugged. It hardly mattered. Like always, he'd get bored while I washed the beast's wound and leave before I'd finished dressing it. If I was lucky, he'd join the others in the guardroom and have a drink, forgetting all about me.

We passed the open room where three other guards played cards, bottles of ale on the floor beside their chairs. They drank while on duty, though never to distraction. My brother's fist wasn't the only thing they invited if they slacked off and got too drunk while they were supposed to be working—as Kengart's face had discovered over a year ago. I'd tended that wound as well, and my stepbrother's knife had cut to the bone. Kengart had been kind to me ever since, as kind as he could be while working under Brunt.

Once we'd passed the guardroom, my footsteps lightened, though it never paid to relax completely. Even in my room, I could only sleep when the door was locked, and my traps were in place.

Kengart moved lazily down the aisle between the cages, not even glancing through the tiny circular windows to see who might be inside. I paused at a few, watching to make sure those I'd helped earlier appeared comfortable and were resting.

"He's in here." Kengart waved to the last cage on the right, the only one without a small, barred window looking out into the hall. He opened the door and stepped inside the dark room with me following. "Looks like he's still unconscious." Trying to see in the dark, I only vaguely heard the concern in Kengart's voice. "Since he's still out of it, I'll leave you alone with him. But call out if you run into trouble."

Many of the beasts could be vicious at first, but this one, like all the others, would sense that I didn't mean harm. Some of the guards called me the beast whisperer because I could walk up to any creature be it tame or wild, and it would never bite. They must be able to tell I would never hurt them.

"Thank you," I said softly, keeping my eyes trained on the dirt floor.

Kengart only remained with me for a moment before stepping back out into the hall.

I waited until his footsteps retreated before shutting the door. None of them were locked. No need to do so when every creature in the cell block was chained.

Taking a whisp lantern from the hook near the door, I blew across it to make it flare. I turned, expecting to find another beast penned in this horrendous place, writhing in pain.

My breath stuttered from my lungs when I spied a wounded orc wearing only a scrap of leather over his groin. He lay on the low bunk mounted to the back wall, a thin blanket covering him to his mid-thighs. Like many in my stepbrother's menagerie, or "pets," as he laughingly called them, the orc was chained at his ankles and wrists. He had enough chain to stand beside the bed and move about, but not enough to reach more than halfway across the small room.

My heart on fire, I watched him, wondering if I dared approach. It was one thing to gently care for a wounded creature, another to go near an orc. Rumors about them crowded out every other thought in my mind. They killed others easily. They were a primitive, nearly feral species. And they captured women and abused them before tossing them aside.

Were the rumors true?

A sheen of sweat covered the green skin of his face and bare, heavily muscled torso, and he thrashed his head, murmuring words I didn't understand. His hair hung about his face and neck in limp, dark strands threaded through with smoky lavender.

I crept closer, taking in the deep laceration on his left shoulder, the big bruise on his temple. More bruises covered his chest, abdomen, and his strong thighs. My heart pinched at the sight. They'd beaten him, probably while capturing him, and from the pus leaking from his wounds, they'd left him untreated from the time they subdued him.

"I'm sorry," I whispered. "You shouldn't be here." Neither should I, but we were both captives in this horrible place.

I lowered my basket to the floor and reached toward him, only to pull my fingers back when he shifted on the bunk, groaning.

His eyes snapped open, and his dark purple gaze clouded with pain met mine.

He wore a metal pendant made up of a five-point star, and as he shifted on the bunk to face me, it slid along the strip of leather encircling his neck.

As if it caught the light from the moon and stars shining down from the night sky so far above this gloomy compound, the pendant blazed.

The orc carefully lifted it, staring in awe as it flickered with light.

"Mate," he growled, his gaze locking on mine. His eyelids fluttered before closing. "Mate."

CHAPTER 2
DAKUR

In my dream, henchmen sent by Madr's cousin snuck up behind me and belted me in the back of the head. I dropped to the ground and rolled, snarling up at them.

They bound me quickly and hefted me, rushing into the woods, taking me far from my clan. Their footsteps barely touched the forest floor as they moved through the woods. My head ached, and the world kept swimming in and out of focus until I passed out.

I woke to hear Madr's cousin bartering with human males, dickering about the price they believed I should fetch. When the coins had been handed over, the cousin and those with him left. I was tossed into a cage mounted on a cart, and bleary-eyed, I studied the other orc locked behind the bars with me. Grock? I believed that was his name. I'd met him only once when he traveled near my land with other members of the Azuris Clan.

He lay much too still on the wooden floor.

An enormous person who appeared to be made up of stone rumbled over to the front of the cart, his footsteps making loud booms on the forest floor. Once the men had climbed onto the long bench spanning the front of the cart, the stone being lifted the bars of metal and trod forward, dragging the cart through the woods, carrying me away from my clan.

With my palms braced on the floorboards, I pushed myself up until I could sit with my legs stretched out before me and my back against the bars of the cage. Pain stabbed through my head, and I clutched it until the world around me stopped spinning. Once I was sure I wouldn't vomit, I leaned over and gently shook Grock's shoulder.

"Wake," I hissed, but he didn't move.

Shifting closer, I listened to his chest and sighed when I didn't hear breathing. A finger against his neck told me his heart had stopped, and his cold skin suggested he'd been dead for a while. The shadow of a bruise covered his right temple, and since I didn't spy any other wounds, I suspected a brain injury was the cause of his death.

"To the wind, the sea, and the mighty trees in the forest, I send your spirit, Grock," I whispered hoarsely, my parched throat telling me I'd been unconscious for a long time. "I will seek vengeance in your name. I'll tell your clan what happened once I'm free and know that I'll seek vengeance for your death."

"Shut up, back there," one of the males barked over his shoulder. "You'll draw predators with your fussing."

While I was tempted to snarl, I saved what little energy I possessed for whatever might come next.

The next morning, they dragged me from the cart, and I fought them as best I could while bound.

They knocked me to the ground and beat me, poking their spears into my hide and bellowing that I'd better behave, or I'd face worse. Wounded and melting in and out of consciousness again, they tossed me inside the cage and left me there.

Sometime later, they sold me to a tall, bald human male who laid me, still trussed up, over the back of a four-legged, horned creature with deep red fur and wild, glowing orange eyes. Its tail whipped up over its spine to smack my back, and I winced, every bone in my body aching.

Once the male had mounted behind me, he snarled when the tail smacked him. "Stop it, beast." A kick of his heels, and the enormous creature lumbered into the forest, taking me from the males who'd purchased me from Madr's cousin.

We rode for days, stopping only to consume scant food and sips of water, which the male reluctantly shared. When he slept at night, he tied me to a tree. There was no chance of escape, and I began to worry about the wounds peppering my chest and thighs, but especially about the large laceration on my shoulder. My wounds festered and seeped, and periodically, my mind whirled around as much as the teetsers that gathered to probe my open skin.

We finally reached the end of the forest and started crossing the desert beyond.

My wounds worsened, and when I lashed out, hoping to escape, the male smacked me in the head with his club. I dropped to my knees with a groan, then tumbled onto my side.

The world went dark, and I didn't wake again until I lay on a hard surface, chained to a stone wall, with a human female staring at me with sweet concern in her beautiful blue eyes.

My pendant flared, and I knew she was mine.

CHAPTER 3
NIA

While the male groaned and shifted on the bed, unconscious once more, I cleansed his wounds that were too numerous to count. It hurt to see him like this. See any of my stepbrother's "pets" like this.

How long before Brunt killed this one?

I mourned each creature who died in the ring, but for some reason, the thought of losing this orc sliced through my belly like a blade. Perhaps because he'd understand why he died where the beasts didn't. They fought due to instinct while the orc was like me. He wasn't human, but he'd understand why he was made to fight, and he'd do so until he died like all the others.

I applied poultices that would beat back the infection and efficiently bound strips of cloth around the large wound on his shoulder. He lay passively beneath my touch, but so did all the beasts I cared for, as if they knew I only meant to help.

It worried me that the orc remained unconscious.

Did the large bruise on his forehead extend into his brain? There wasn't anything I could do about swelling there. It would kill him no matter how much I struggled to help.

Would he survive long enough to be tossed into my stepbrother's ring to fight, or would he succumb to the infection or a head injury?

Only time would tell.

After I'd finished with his cuts and bruises, applying a soothing balm to all, I straightened, pressing my hand against my spasming lower back. Staring down at him, I knew I should leave. He was sleeping, and hopefully he'd sleep long enough to begin healing. He didn't need me watching over him for that.

He shifted on the bed, his head turning slightly my way, and he groaned, shoving the light blanket I'd covered him with all the way down to his waist. When I was treating him, he was a patient. I saw him, but I didn't actually *see* him.

Now I did.

I'd been around men most of my life. It was hard to miss them when my stepfather ran a smithy and other assorted businesses. While my stepfather was around, they were polite to me. It was only when he died, and my stepbrother took over the businesses, that hands would wander too close, and gazes would lock on my frame in a way that made me shudder.

The only orcs I'd seen were at a distance were huge, hulking males carrying weapons twice the size of those hefted by Brunt's men.

From the way his feet hung over the end of the bunk, this orc male was tall. He'd tower over everyone around him—in the village, at least. And broad, with rippling muscles shifting smoothly beneath his green skin flecked with so many scars, he must've seen an incredible amount of battle in the past.

He was a warrior unlike any other.

I took in his strong jawline that appeared crafted from the enormous slabs of granite the men hauled on carts to be sliced for stoops and foundations. His tusks jutted up from his lower jaw, and I bet he could use his enormous hands to hold prey while he ripped into it with his tusks.

I should shudder and step away from him, but just looking at him sparked something deep within me, in a place that had never been touched by anyone but me.

His hair tumbled around his shoulders, and from when it had brushed against my hands while I assessed his neck, I remembered it was silker than I'd ever imagined. Even now, I had the urge to glide my fingers through the dark strands threaded through with smoky lavender.

Fetching a basin of water, I dipped a clean cloth in and wrung it out. I stooped beside his bed and gently cleansed his face, removing the dirt and flecks of blood. I suspected some of it wasn't from him but those he'd battled to avoid capture or while trying to escape.

I knew no one would ever be able to permanently pin this brawny orc down.

It hurt that he was as trapped here as me. He seemed

wild and untamed, a person who should never be bound by chains and the cruelty of my stepbrother.

Someone passed in the hall, their heavy footsteps dull thuds, and my fingers froze in the orc's hair.

Seeing that it was as soiled as the rest of him, I fetched more clean water and another cloth and did the best I could, running the wet fabric along clumps of his hair numerous times. After, I gently finger combed it and secured it at his nape with a strip of fabric. I even rubbed dirt and blood off his horns, thick things that jutted from his skull above each temple.

He groaned when I touched them, so I left them alone after that, watching until he'd slipped away into what I hoped were good dreams once more. Everyone deserved an escape, and if he could find a bit of peace in his rest, I was glad for him.

Too soon, his life would become a living nightmare.

I fetched yet another basin of clean water. His broad chest got equal attention, and I tried not to stare when his nipples puckered at my touch. My face heated, and the tingling I'd felt deep within me bloomed, spreading warmth to that secret place between my legs.

I kept expecting Kengart to return, or one of the other guards to step inside the room and tell me the orc who'd soon die in the arena could do that as easily dirty as clean. When they didn't, I sat beside him and continued washing, slowly gliding the cloth across his taut abdomen with muscles ripping in broad bands, all the way down to his groin.

There, I didn't quite dare venture. I left his loincloth

in place and covered his chest with the coarse blanket, focusing on his thighs thick with rippling muscles. Each had its own definition, and with every glide of my damp cloth, electric jolts shot through me until I was breathing as if I'd raced through the village, my pulse a furious rampage in my throat.

My lips parted as I continued lower, gently lifting his legs to cleanse his equally firm calves and feet that twitched at my touch. I kept shooting glances at his face, but he didn't wake.

Only his pendant responded, blazing like an energetic whisp I'd blown across multiple times. Did the star-shaped disk contain its own kind of light?

Finally, I couldn't linger with him any longer. I wanted to sit beside him, and I felt oddly compelled to hold his hand and stroke his brow, to tell him everything would be all right.

Instead, I dumped the water and returned to my room.

THE NEXT DAY, I returned to the cells, making my rounds. I spent nearly an hour talking a pair of ashenclaws into letting me come near. The ferocious, furred creatures much like enormous, wild dogs, had fought in the arena the night before and each received wounds that needed tending.

The tops of their shoulders came to my mid-chest, and thick chains pinned them to the back wall of their cage. They could barely reach their water and plate of food, plus the pad placed on the floor for sleeping.

"It's all right," I said softly as I approached them with my fingers extended. My eyes stung with tears. My stepbrother was much too cruel, too heartless. How could he force such majestic creatures to fight when they only deserved to be free?

Finally, the largest of the pair allowed me to come close enough to touch his fuzzy cheek. He even nudged my side with his long furry snout and huffed as I carefully washed his wounds and applied ointment that would aid in healing.

After tending to them both, I gently brushed their thick, ash gray fur that gave them their name, and carefully clipped the half-torn claw on the smaller beast, a female. Were they a mated pair?

I'd do what I could to free them. If I could sneak them from their cell when the guards weren't looking, I could guide them to the desert. After that, I could only hope they'd run so far away, Brunt would never find them again. Tonight, I'd see what I could do. Until then, I'd tell Brunt they weren't up to fighting, that they were both too injured to last for more than a few moments in the ring—an excuse that worked about half the time.

"I'll be back," I whispered, gathering my things.

When I slipped from their cage, I found Kengart leaving the one across the hall.

"Who's in there?" I asked.

"A creature you'll need to leave alone." Sweat trickled

down his brow, and his clothing was torn in places. "It's vicious, I tell you. Stay away."

"Are you wounded?" I lifted my basket.

"I'll wash and be fine. Go along with you now."

Lifting my chin, I stared him down. "If the creature's hurt, I need to examine it."

"Not this one." He scratched the back of his neck and gaped at the slash on his left hand as if he only now saw it. His swear ripped out. "I need to go take care of this before it festers."

I handed him a tiny pot of ointment with a sigh. "Put this on it and it'll heal faster."

"You're too kind for this place, Nia," he said curtly. "Too good for this world in general." This was one of the few times he'd said anything nice to me. Brunt's staff universally snarled at me.

Or tried to grope me.

"I do what I can." I peered toward the door of the cage he'd left.

His gaze followed mine. "I mean it. This one's too mean even for you. Brunt put it there last night and . . ." He shook his head. "Leave it alone."

"What is it?"

"Some kind of beast from a land far from here. Never seen anything like it before in my life. It's big." His hand rose almost to his shoulder-level. "Its glowing red eyes make your skin crawl. How the fates created such a creature is beyond me. It's nearly impossible to kill with its long claws, scaled hide, and sweeping tail that could impale you if you're not quick on your feet."

"It sounds intimidating." But still, if it was injured, I'd do what I could. I hadn't met a creature yet that wouldn't let me near it.

"Stay away. This one will fight soon, though I think Brunt's saving it for a special match. He'll talk it up, and I bet people will even come from the city to see it fight and rip some poor soul apart. He'll make a lot of money, he will."

And that was Brunt's sole purpose in life: to amass more wealth.

"Tend to the orc," Kengart said, nudging his head in that direction. "He was stirring. He'll be in the arena soon, and I'm looking forward to watching. I've never seen an orc fight, though I've heard they're nearly impossible to kill." A sneer rose on his face. "Not sure if I'll bet for or against him, though I heard he put up quite a fight after he was captured."

Yes, and that was when he was wounded. Who could blame him for trying to keep from being taken?

"I'll go to him now." Without speaking further, I took my basket down the hall with Kengart following. He opened the door, waving for me to enter.

"You want me there to poke him with my blade? That'll show him he needs to behave. Might keep him from threatening you."

I gave him a brow-lifted look.

He had the good sense to back away. "All right. I understand. You prefer to tend to the wounded without anyone else there to watch over you."

This was the policy I'd stuck to since I allowed a

guard to "help" me with a beast, and he'd killed the creature he saw as a threat. Truly, the beast hadn't threatened me, though he had snarled at the guard, no doubt because the guard had caused the creature pain.

"Call out if you need me, then." After staring at the orc lying still on the bed, Kengart pivoted on his heel and strode out of the cage, heading to the break room where someone was already calling out the number on their cards. He'd soon be entrenched in a game and would leave me alone.

After quietly closing the door, I crept across the room and stared down at the orc. Like yesterday when I'd carefully washed his body, a warm hum rose inside me, centering low in my belly. I didn't know what it meant, and frankly, it scared me.

Was I attracted to this orc? Only pain would come from emotions like that. He wouldn't live long enough for me to feel more for him than any of the others.

Sitting beside him with my basket of tinctures and herbs by my feet, I stroked his forehead, telling myself that I was trying to determine if he had a fever, though I enjoyed touching him more than I should.

Again, his skin was softer than I'd expected, though I didn't believe I'd ever contemplated how an orc's skin might feel. And his hair felt incredibly soft when I gently ran my fingers behind his nape—telling myself I was making sure there were no bumps or swollen areas on the back of his head, though I'd already catalogued all his wounds the day before and found none there.

When I couldn't find another excuse to touch him, I

carefully lifted the edges of his bandages to examine his wounds, finding them healing much faster than a human.

Stunned, I studied his face, though his eyelids remained closed, and he didn't appear to be aware I was near. How had he healed so quickly?

It was clear he didn't need any care from me today. I could change his bandages tomorrow, though if he kept healing at this rate, he wouldn't need to have his wounds covered after that. I stood and leaned against the cold stone wall beside the head of his bed.

I was watching him. Not leaving to tend to others.

He slept, his chest rising and falling gently, and the hard shell I'd placed around my heart whenever I treated one of my stepbrother's pets cracked. I should shore it up, make sure the structure I built around it was impenetrable. This orc would die like the rest of the poor souls trapped in this compound. Knowing this made everything inside me hurt as if I was the one taking the blows.

I swallowed past my tight throat and swiped at my eyes that shouldn't be wet. Yet I was sad. At least the creatures I tended didn't know what was coming.

This orc soon would.

Peering around the cage, I took inventory of the bucket in the corner for waste, another nearby with water he could drink, and a metal table screwed to the wall with a hunk of bread sitting on it. Not even a plate for presentation, and definitely no meat or cheese. I'd get some and leave it for him, plus a mug for water.

He'd need protein to heal and get strong, and he

wasn't a beast like the others who were content to eat out of a trough and drink from the bucket, though they were sentient creatures as much as this orc. No, he felt different when he shouldn't.

I knew nothing about orcs other than those brief glimpses I'd had of them in the desert, though from what I'd heard in the village, they were not only ferocious; they were smart. Fierce. And loyal to their clans.

Would any of them come looking for this orc?

"Where do you come from?" I whispered.

His eyes opened, and he stared up at me with a look in his eyes I couldn't define. It delved deep within me as if he was staring at my very soul.

My breath caught, and my heart flipped over. Tingles shot down my spine, and I straightened, gasping.

When his pendant blazed with light again, he placed his palm over it, his gaze still locked with mine.

"Mate," he murmured. "What is your name, pretty one?"

"I'm anything but pretty." Before I could stop myself, I ran my fingertips down the network of scars on my face, cringing as I expected him to do.

"Pretty one," he said, his voice deep and rumbly.

Was he mocking me? The kind look in his eyes said no, but what did I know of males other than the men my stepbrother employed? Each would happily take advantage of me if they didn't fear Brunt's hand rising to strike.

He didn't protect me from his men because he cared. No, he was saving me for something else. I'd sensed this since I fully matured. It was only a matter of time before he acted on his plan.

I wasn't sure why this orc had used the term mate, but there was no harm in telling him my name. It held no power. "I'm Nia."

"And I'm Dakur of the Matis Clan."

DAKUR

"Dakur," she whispered, the sound of her voice making heat flare deep within me, as if only this female held the spark that would ever ignite me.

My fated mate was human, and she was the loveliest being I'd ever seen. She was so tiny I doubted the top of her head would reach past my elbow. And my fellow warriors would gasp at her strangely pale hair and light blue eyes. She had lush breasts I ached to touch, and a plump ass and frame that would be treasured by every single male in my clan.

And she didn't think she was pretty?

Hating that I was lying on a bunk in what looked like a prison cell while my mate studied me as intently as I did her, I struggled to rise. Chains jangled at my wrists and ankles, and I grimaced at the manacles binding me to them. I was strong, but I doubted I had the strength to break them.

While I'd studied her, she'd inched toward the barred

door, but she rushed forward and supported me in my efforts to sit on the side of the bed.

I also hated that I was panting by the time I sat leaning against the stone wall with my legs extended.

"Don't push yourself. Not yet," she said, her eyes meeting mine. Her very soul shone there, and it reflected her inner beauty.

"Why did you say you're not pretty?"

She stiffened and reeled back from me. Her hand rose to her face again, and her cheeks pinkened. "Don't mock me."

The cratering of her voice made me want to hold her, but I doubted she'd welcome the gesture. "I would never do something like that."

"I have scars," she said, her eyes sparkling with tears, though her chin lifted. "If I was ever pretty, I no longer am."

"What happened?"

"My . . ." Her gaze darted toward the door, and she lowered her voice to a low hiss. "My stepfather and mother died in a fire. I escaped, though not completely."

"A fire?"

"Someone started it. No one knows who."

"I'll kill them," I growled, shooting to my feet and nearly passing out from my efforts.

"I said no one knows who did it, so it would be hard for you to track them down and kill them." She nudged me toward the side of the bunk. "Sit before you undo my efforts."

I took in the neat bandages on my wounds. "Orcs heal fast."

Her frown traveled to the wound on my shoulder that had started to bleed through the bandage. "Not fast enough."

I let her help me settle once more, my lips twitching upward when she hefted my legs one by one to gently lay them on the hard surface. It was all she could do to lift them.

"Let me look at your shoulder," she said with a huff. "You need to lay still and give yourself time to heal."

Leaning against the wall again in a semi-upright position, I watched as she carefully peeled back the bandage, exposing a gash longer than my hand. It seeped, but it didn't appear deep, not any longer. I'd moved my shoulder since receiving it, and while it got infected, everything inside worked as it should.

"It was a deep wound, but with time, it'll fully heal." Her gaze darted to mine, and she was so close, I could catch her floral scent with one sniff.

If I leaned forward, I could capture her lips with my own.

My pendant flared, reminding me that my clan's fates had chosen this female over every other as my perfect match.

And it appeared I'd met my fated one in a prison.

"Yes, you have scars on your face," I said softly, as gently as I could. Like an elkern, I worried she'd startle if I attempted to touch her.

Her fingers stilled on my body before she continued

applying a fresh poultice to the wound. It felt better already. Her touch was kind and caring. "They extend down my neck as well, you'll note."

"As *you* may note, my body is riddled with scars."

"You're a warrior."

"I sense you're a warrior as well."

She scoffed and tugged a roll of bandage from the basket she'd placed beside my bed. "I've never seen battle."

"Haven't you?" When she didn't look up, I tilted her chin, locking her gaze with mine. "I believe you've seen your share of fights."

"I've never lifted a sword."

"You didn't gain your scars in a fight, but you suffered as much, if not more than me, when you obtained them."

"They hurt horribly," she said with only the shadow of a voice. "But nowhere as bad as my heart at the loss of my mom and stepfather."

"I'm sorry. I wish I'd been here to protect you. To help you and your parents escape."

Her eyes pinched shut for only a moment. "Thank you."

"Never feel your scars are unsightly. They're a symbol of strength and perseverance."

"That's not what everyone in the village says. They call me a monster."

"Then they're fools."

Her face lightened, and her lips twitch upward in the prettiest smile I'd ever seen. "Now you're teasing me."

"I only tell the truth."

"No one tells the truth entirely. They only tell shades of whatever they wish you to believe."

How had this gentle female survived in such a place as this?

With the strength and perseverance I'd just named. I sensed she'd made herself find a way because the thought of doing anything else was abhorrent.

"I'm not just a warrior, I'm a caedos," I said. "We try very hard to always tell the truth."

"*Caedos.*" She frowned as her gaze met mine before she returned her attention to my wound. "I don't know the term."

"It's a position in my clan—the Matis Clan. We live deep in a forest."

"I've never seen a forest, just the spindly trees growing around the body of water near our village."

"There are so many trees there, no one could count them."

"Is it hot there? Sunny all the time?"

"We see all seasons, though it never gets too cold. It's cool in the summer, partly due to the shade the trees provide, and if it gets too cold in the winter, we lounge in the hot pools in caves deep below the ground."

"It's so hot here all the time, I can't imagine ever wishing to sit in a hot pool." She shook her head and gave me another smile I'd treasure forever. "I'd sweat." She finished retying the bandage and nodded pertly. "You need to lie still and give this time to clot again. New ones here in the holding area aren't given much time to recover, but I'll tell my stepbrother you're still too injured to battle. He paid a pretty coin for you, I'm sure, and he won't want to lose it during your first fight."

"Where am I?"

"In the lower level of my stepbrother, Brunt's, compound in our village. The village was built near an oasis in the middle of the desert many generations ago. There's a human city far from here and a few other villages, but I've never traveled to any of them. They're too far and it's too dangerous crossing the desert."

"Fight you said." Her words made my heart grew colder than the snow we scraped off our platforms in the worst part of winter.

Her gaze darted up to meet mine. "My stepbrother buys creatures, and now you, an orc, to throw into a ring to fight. He takes bets and makes a lot of money. He's uncanny at choosing those who can survive the longest against the harshest odds."

This was her only surviving relative? My poor mate.

"The creatures and a few people are held in cages in this lower level," she said. "But deeper, you'll find a large arena. It's there that they gather to watch fights and place bets."

"I was sold to battle in this arena like in gladiator tournaments I've heard of a few times before."

"Yes. I'm sorry." Her attention darted to the door. "I can't remain with you much longer. They'll come looking for me."

"Who?"

"The guards. Kengart brought me to your cell, but the others will come with him."

"To protect you."

Her sigh bled out. "No, to touch me if they think they can get away with it."

A snarl ripped up my throat. I would kill them—all of them—if I could get my hands on them.

"Above this level, you'll find the top part of the compound that holds a kitchen and dining area, some rooms including mine, and Brunt's office. The village is called Woobedon."

"Desert. Have you heard of the Ember Clan?"

"No. I don't know of clans and there's no other village nearby. I've lived here my entire life and if such a place existed, I would've heard of it. As for orcs, I've only seen them at a distance in the desert. They never come to the village. They . . ."

"What?"

She shrugged. "I'm beginning to think most of the rumors I heard about orcs aren't true."

I'd heard them all, and I assumed the ones she referred to were complete lies. "We don't harm others. We're mostly a peaceful people."

"You don't act like what I've heard." Her gaze fell on my mouth. "You have tusks."

My laugh burst out. "All orcs have tusks."

"Do they get in the way when you eat?" Her attention remained there.

I couldn't help but run my tongue across my lips. "No more than the rest of my teeth."

"What about when you kiss someone?" She burst to her feet, and for a moment, I worried someone was coming, someone who would hurt her while I wasn't in a position to defend her. "I'm sorry." She rushed to the door but halted there, her back to me. "I shouldn't have asked something as forward as that."

"I haven't kissed anyone," I blurted out. If only she'd stay with me. Talk with me.

Turning, she frowned. "You're handsome. Why not?"

"Because I was waiting for you, my precious mate."

CHAPTER 5

NIA

"You shouldn't say such things," I whispered, my hand on the knob. If I was wise, I'd rush from here and never return. Not to this cell, that is. He'd heal from my care, and if I remained with him much longer, the feelings growing in my heart for him would only get stronger. I hadn't been with anyone sexually, but I knew what the heat simmering low in my belly meant.

It was hard enough watching a beast I'd tended to die in the arena. It would be utterly devastating to learn that Dakur had been killed.

"I apologize," he said. "You've been kind. I'm an orc, and you're a—"

"Don't." Turning, I leaned against the door. "Never think I don't want you to kiss me."

"Then—"

Without giving him a chance to finish, I opened the door and shut it behind me. I fled down the hall, rushing past the open guard doorway where Brunt's men still played cards, washing down their sputtering conversation with weak ale.

They were busy . . .

As wound up as I was, there was something I wanted to take care of. I tiptoed back and carefully lifted the keys from the peg by the guardroom, taking care not to let the keys clink together. I slipped past the room once more and went to the cage holding the ashenclaws.

They rose when I entered, and I patted them for a moment before unlocking their metal collars.

"Come with me, sweet ones," I said in a soothing voice, urging them toward the door of the cage. I peeked into the hall before grabbing their ruffs and leading them to the right. We traveled through the halls, the pads of their feet silent and mine a subtle whisper.

I eased them around the arena, shuddering when I caught a glance of the stained sand coating the central area.

On the other side, I led the beasts up the ramp, all the way to the top, and I breathed a sigh of relief when I didn't find a guard on duty. During the games, Brunt kept this area guarded. Everyone who attended the event must pay. He'd never allow anyone to sneak in without handing over a coin.

Sultry air greeted us, and I stopped to listen before leading the ashenclaws to the left. Before I reached the end of the street, they burst past me, heading toward the open desert beyond the edge of the village.

Only when their paws were sinking in the sand did they turn back. The male dipped his head my way while the female whined. I waved, and they spun around and raced toward freedom.

With a sigh but a happier heart, I hurried back the way I came, returned the key, then rushed up the stairs.

I didn't slow until I'd nearly reached my room. Outside my door, I paused, listening. When I didn't hear anyone nearby, I opened my door slowly, watching as the tiny slip of fabric I'd wedged at knee-height between the panel and the frame fluttered to the floor.

If it was no longer there, it would mean someone had opened the door and was perhaps waiting inside.

Brunt, of course. Few others would dare.

But since the fabric was still in place, it was safe to enter my room.

Inside, I shut and locked the door, wedging two blocks of wood into the gap between the door and the jamb. At least three times in the past few months, I'd awakened to someone carefully testing the lock. One of them had even shoved his shoulder against the panel. It shuddered but held. I wasn't confident the lock would keep anyone out if they were truly determined to get inside, so I'd added the wedges.

I'd laid awake for hours after the last attempt, unable to sleep, and tiredness had clawed at my eyes all the next day. No one looked at me any differently than usual, and I wasn't sure who'd tried to get inside, but this told me I needed to leave the compound forever.

I had no idea where I'd go, but I'd soon have to flee and take my chances in the desert just like the ashenclaws.

Fleeing presented a variety of problems without solutions.

Could I find a job in the village? My skills in the kitchen and with healing would be in demand, but would anyone dare hire me when they believed I belonged to Brunt? I worried they wouldn't, and I'd have to drag myself back to the compound and beg his forgiveness—or starve.

Did I dare try crossing the desert alone? I wasn't sure in which direction to head, though I'd heard of a city far to the east and a vast forest to the north.

I was saving each coin I collected for the herbs and simple poultices I crafted, but it was nowhere near enough to buy the supplies I'd need for what was probably a few weeks' trek across the sand.

If and when I fled, I'd have to make sure no one followed.

The door wedges wouldn't hold someone back if they were determined to get inside, so I'd long since started using other methods to at least alert me.

I stood on a chair near the room's sole window and ran a bit of string through the ring I'd attached to the ceiling. I hung two pieces of metal I'd pierced with holes and allowed them to dangle. Once I'd attached the other end of the string to the window that could only be opened by being lifted, I carefully secured the string above the pieces of metal to a hook on the side of the window. If someone jimmied the lock and raised the glass, the string would slip from the hook and the metal would jangle together when it swung, waking me.

Not that I slept well to begin with.

As a final measure, I propped a shallow metal bowl on the top of the doorknob then gently placed tiny bells I'd purchased in town inside the depression. If someone turned the knob, the bowl would fall off and hit the floor. The bells would ring out, waking me.

It was a wonder I slept at all.

I curled on my bed and tugged up the blankets, wishing I was far from here, someplace safe. Did such a place exist?

For the first time in my life, I pictured someone with me in that wonderful place—Dakur. I was foolish to dream of a new life, let alone of someone to share it with, especially someone who'd be dead soon.

But my mom had taught me to dream, and what harm was there in that?

No one would know but me.

I woke the next morning to a bang on the door. "Better scurry there, Nia," Veegar hissed through the panel. "Brunt's awake, and he's angry."

I froze. Had he discovered I'd released the ashenclaws? He couldn't know it was me.

Skittish, I rose and washed in the basin, donning my usual garb, a skirt that brushed across my ankles and a loose blouse. They'd belonged to my mother. If they hadn't been with the washer woman during the fire, I'd have nothing.

After dismantling my window alarm and setting the bowl of bells on a table, I removed the wedges and unlocked the door, making sure I was alone before venturing out into the hall.

I spent a lot of time working in the below-ground cells healing creatures and now an orc, but when my stepbrother brought me here after the fire, he told me I must work for my room and board, that nothing would be freely provided.

I hurried into the kitchen and as Veegar kneaded dough, I took a large chicken from the cold box where I'd placed it yesterday after purchasing it in the market. I put it in the largest pot we had, added water and a few spices, and turned on the heat to bring it to a boil. I'd simmer it for hours then pick the bones clean, reserving some of the broth to make gravy for tomorrow's meal, but saving most of it for a soup.

While Veegar formed mounds of bread and placed them in pans to rise, I washed and chopped vegetables, placing them in a bowl to add to my broth later.

After turning the burner down to a low simmer, I got four dozen eggs out of the pantry and started cracking them, dumping the insides in a bowl to scramble.

"Food," Brunt bellowed from the dining area.

Veegar gave it right back to him in a snarl. "It'll be there when it's ready." Only he dared speak like that to Brunt. I sure didn't. The one time my stepbrother backhanded Veegar for talking back, Veegar strode through the back door and didn't return.

I'd held my grin while Brunt's men berated him for

driving Veegar away, and it wasn't long before Brunt was making promises to behave—with Veegar, that is. I could leave if he hit me, but Veegar had family who'd take him in. I had no place to go, and I didn't quite dare try to make my way on the streets. Everyone knew what women had to do to survive out there, and I wasn't ready to give that career a try.

I cooked the eggs while Veegar sliced yesterday's bread and fried it in butter, piling the thick, hot slices on big platters. My belly roared at the wonderful smell, but there'd be no food for me until everyone else was served.

With my arms loaded with platters of bread and eggs, I butted the door between the dining area and the kitchen open and hurried to the central table. I kept my eyes down as I lowered the platters and scurried out of reach of roaming hands.

Brunt scowled when one of his men smacked my ass.

"Leave her alone," he barked, and the guy hung his head.

Back in the kitchen, I reloaded my hands and brought that food into the dining area, too, making sure there was enough for the eighteen men bellied up to the tables. My stepbrother not only ran the only gambling establishment in town—the arena—but he also owned the smithy where they crafted tools and weapons, plus the only carpentry shop in the village. There, his men made furniture, though a few also constructed and repaired buildings. Both businesses had belonged to my stepfather, and Brunt had inherited them when his father died. Before that, Brunt only owned the glassmaker's shop.

My mother had done well to marry such a wealthy man, and she once told me my dowry would be large enough to command the attention of a lord. As far as I knew, there weren't any lords in the village. The highest-ranking official was the mayor, and he was already married. But what did I know? Maybe she'd dreamed of traveling to the city and introducing me there.

It didn't matter any longer. Brunt had no intention of marrying me off to anyone, not when he benefited from my labor.

While the pans soaked for washing, I ate eggs and a slice of bread. After, Veegar prepped for the lunch meal, and I rushed into the dining room and started collecting dirty dishes. I'd wash everything and finish helping Veegar make lunch. Since dinner was already started, I'd have some "free" time after the lunch hour, though I'd use it to check on my patients in the cells and collect more herbs in the low hills near the oasis.

I found the dining room empty except for Brunt. There was nothing unusual about that. He often sat and savored his tea after the others had left.

Seeing me, he pointed to the chair on his right. He'd taken the head of the table as usual. "Sit."

I paused three chairs down, gripping the back of it, the muscles in my legs bunched to leap if I had to. "Is there something you need?" I kept my tone light. I didn't want to rile him up without just cause.

"Sit, I said."

Fighting on this would do me no good, so I slipped into the seat, keeping my eyes trained on the table.

"The ashenclaws escaped," he said softly.

My breath caught before I could still my actions. "Is that so?"

"You wouldn't happen to have had anything to do with that, would you?"

Death lurked in his voice. If I admitted anything, that death would find me quickly.

"Of course not," I said as calmly as possible. Hopefully, he wouldn't notice I trembled.

"You better not have been involved. You know what happens to those who cost me money."

"Yes," I said in a tiny voice.

A long silence followed, but I didn't look up at him. Maybe he'd dismiss me now and I could run. Hide in my room for a bit.

"I've been thinking about your future, Nia," he finally said.

My heart stalled, then flopped around, but I just bit into my lower lip and nodded.

"My father had grand ideas for a wealthy marriage for you, one that would add to his power, and he was a wise man, my father."

"Yes, he was. Kind too." I didn't point out that he'd truly cared for me, unlike Brunt.

"While I, too, could benefit with increased power, I'm not sure who I should give you to."

I swallowed the lump of fear in my throat and tightened my spine. "I belong to myself. There will be no giving me to anyone."

"You can't remain unwed."

"Why not?"

"The mayor came to visit and pointed out that your reputation will be in ruins if you remain here, living among so many men."

"I have my own room."

"Which I could fill with another worker once you were married or, perhaps, one who'd share your bed."

"Who are you thinking of?" The words came out in a croak.

His sly grin rose. "I'm not quite sure yet."

"Please don't marry me to anyone."

"You belong to me," he growled. "Every female in the village is a possession of the male head of a household."

"That's not true. You're not my blood relative." My fingers tightened on my lap to the point of blanching.

"You were young when your mother married my father."

"Twelve." Ten years ago.

"You reached maturity at least four years ago. I should've married you off right then."

"Your father told me I'd have some say in who I wed." My voice shook, but I was having a hard time seeing my way out of this tenuous situation. I needed to save money for at least a few more months before I'd have enough to make my way in the world.

"He's dead. I control your future now." Anger churned in his voice. He'd never liked it when someone didn't immediately agree with whatever he said. "You listen to me. You do as I say. The mayor's brother is interested."

"He's twice my age." And he'd already overworked and buried three wives.

"I'd only let him have you if he gave me enough to cover your duties here for at least the next few years. I don't like to lose out."

That was an incredible amount of money.

"So far," he added, toying with his eating implement, banging it against his plate in a steady clang that grated on my nerves. "He's still thinking about it, but he might be convinced. Another option is to give you to Lianire, but he doesn't have enough coin to pay the price I'm asking." His hand snapped out and latched onto my wrist. "You haven't let anyone between your legs, have you? I'm telling anyone offering that you're pure and untouched." His sneer rose as his gaze dropped from mine to my face. "Other than the scars, that is, but in the dark, most men don't care what a woman looks like as long as she spreads her thighs wide and lets him do as he pleases."

"I haven't been with anyone," I said in a tiny voice.

For whatever reason, my mind shot to Dakur. Whoever my brother gave me to would use me as hard in the bedroom as he would in the kitchen.

I sensed Dakur would be gentle, though I had no reason to believe this other than from our short interaction. He'd offered me a kiss. *Offered*, not demanded. Perhaps that was why I believed he'd treat me sweetly.

Believing he'd survive long enough to even kiss me was a foolish thought on my part. He'd be dead within days. He'd never be in a position to rescue me.

If I was going to get out of this situation, I'd have to do so myself.

"Lianire prefers males," I pointed out.

"He likes both, and he's interested in having children. He could get it up enough to plant one each year, and then he'd still have himself a good worker when he has enough children." Brunt frowned down at his plate. "But he also must pay a good price if he wants me to pick him."

Telling Brunt I wouldn't marry anyone I didn't choose myself would only get me a smack on the arm or side, and it would sting for hours.

"How long will you keep looking for my husband?" I asked.

"Ten days." He rose. "Then I'm going to hold an auction."

"An auction?" I gasped, my eyes shooting his way.

"That would be best. We can drive up the bidding to the point everyone's feverish to win." Lifting a package off the table, he tossed it at me.

Catching it, I stared down at it blankly, unable to comprehend being part of something as horrifying as an auction for my hand in marriage.

"Open it," Brunt barked.

After placing it on the table, I unwrapped the string tie and put the string in my pocket. I never threw anything away that might be useful in my escape, something I was going to have to put into place much sooner than I'd expected.

When I unfolded the cloth wrapping, I found something that, under any other circumstances, might make me smile.

"Nice, huh?" he said like a proud, indulgent guardian. "Hold it up against yourself and see what you think."

Knowing he'd make me if I didn't cooperate, I stood and lifted the red silk gown, realizing then how daring it was. I gaped down at the low neckline and snug bodice. The skirt flared at the waist, and I knew it would fit me perfectly. Brunt had watched me enough to figure out my size.

"It's a gown," I said dully.

"Hold it against yourself," he snarled, not liking that I wasn't bouncing around the room with excitement. "You'll wear it at the auction."

I didn't have to ask why. He'd fetch a high price for someone dressed in something as seductive as this. It was all I could do not to shout that I'd never do it.

Long ago, I would've.

Now I bided my time, trying to avoid inciting his anger to the point where he might injure me to keep me from breaking free.

"The men will go wild when they see you wearing that," he said. "Personally, I believe the mayor's brother will be the highest bidder. He's the wealthiest of the bunch. So don't you worry, sister, I'm sure we'll have you matched up with the right man soon enough."

"What if none of them make a high enough offer?" Would he drag me to the city and set up an auction there?

"That's a good question." Rising, he strode around

me while I stared blankly at the dress slumped in my hands.

He walked to the door leading to the front room, no doubt planning to go to his office beyond. But he stopped in the opening, turning back. "I guess if they don't bid high enough, I'll see what else they're willing to offer. Some of the interested men own businesses, and I could take a share. No matter what, you'll be wed to one of them in ten days."

"I won't be given time to prepare for my wedding?" I asked in a shaky voice. I didn't care about a gown or any sort of celebration; I just wanted more time.

"You'll wed the highest bidder that night. I imagine he'll be eager to solidify the union."

I stood in the dining room after he left, my body a complete wreck. I couldn't make my heart stop thundering in my ears, and my breathing raged as if I'd run all the way across the village.

If only I *could* run.

My eyes stung with tears as I bound up the dress and rewrapped it. I'd toss it in my room and if I had my say, I'd never wear it.

I mechanically gathered the rest of the dishes and took them to the kitchen, where I washed the pans in the sink, then refilled it with clean water, letting more dishes soak while I scrubbed off the tables.

Veegar watched me more intently than usual, but he didn't say a word.

When all the dishes were done, I finished the lunch prep and hid some leftovers in a square of cloth when

Veegar wasn't looking. Holding it and the dress, I hurried from the kitchen.

"I'll be back later," I said gruffly.

"Yup," Veegar said with a heavy sigh.

Inside my room, I stuffed the dress beneath my bed and gathered what I needed.

With my basket of medicinal supplies hanging over my arm, I descended into the lower level, pausing every few steps to listen. Only the occasional thud of footsteps or a grumbling voice reached my ears, and I continued to the bottom.

Like always when I came to this area, I crept through the hallway as quiet as a mouse.

CHAPTER 6
DAKUR

I woke and sat up to practice.

Long before I was destined to be the caedos, or leader, of my clan, I'd wanted to be a wanderer, one of a small group of orcs who traveled the world seeking new ways to use the gift from our fates.

Since taking up the mantle after my father's death, I'd had to put that dream aside. I was too busy with the everyday tasks of running my clan. Had my skills grown rusty?

Lying on my bunk, I lifted my pendant and gently blew across it, creating a low hum that vibrated through my bones. A whisp lantern hanging near the door burst into light almost as bright as my pendant had flared when I first met Nia.

My smile made the cuts on my face ache.

I noted my arms weren't dirty like they had been before I was sold. Had someone bathed me?

My heart cratered to think it was Nia. I doubted there

was anyone else in this wretched place possessing her kindness, her caring.

Knowing she was an ally heartened me, and I tested a few more puffs of air across my pendant, trialing those I'd learned when I was much younger than now.

Some might call this magic, but all wanderers knew that varying tones could change the very world around us. It was a gift from the fates to my clan, and each of us cherished it.

I practiced, and my skills tightened until I could make the blanket draw itself up over my chest and clumps of dirt on the floor skitter across until they reached the wall.

Sitting, I blew again, and the bucket of water scraped closer until I could scoop out water with the mug left on the table. I drank the brackish liquid that was better than nothing.

Exhausted, I moved the bucket back and laid down on my bunk, satisfied with what I'd done so far. I'd keep practicing and trialing new tones, and soon, I'd have better control over the world around me.

I must've dozed, because I awoke to someone opening my door. I stilled myself and kept my breathing even.

A person slid into the room, and the panel snicked shut behind them.

It was only when Nia laid her soft hand on my forehead that I opened my eyes.

Relief filled her pretty face, her eyes glowing brighter

than my pendant. "You're not unconscious," she whispered. "I wasn't sure."

I shook my head, unsure if I dared speak because her words were barely audible. Did she worry someone might be listening?

I nodded.

"I was worried." Her voice lifted, telling me she wasn't concerned about being overheard after all. Only then did my posture loosen and did I loosen my grip on the metal bar lying close to my thigh. I'd slowly pried it off the metal table overnight, leaving the structure leaning against the wall on three legs. It took hours to break it free, but at least I had a weapon. When the orcs sent by the king's nephew initially grabbed me and clubbed my head, I'd staggered and dropped to my knees. They'd ripped my mace from my hand and chucked it into the woods along with all my blades.

"I'm fine," I said. More than fine. Because I was so happy to see her, my smile rose. "I told you orcs heal quickly."

Her answering smile fell flat. "You need to pretend you're still horribly injured."

"For how long?"

Biting down on her lower lip, she shot a glance at the door. "Until I can come up with a plan to help us escape."

I should be the one making escape plans, not her. But I liked that she saw us together even if it was only to find our way free of this trap.

"I brought you some food." She tugged a small packet from her basket and held it out to me.

It crushed me that, again, she was doing something for me when I was helpless to do anything for her.

"Thank you." I sat up on the bed, leaning against the wall as she laid her offering on my lap. "You know there's an old orc saying that if a lovely female offers an orc a meal crafted by her very hands, she's giving him her heart."

Nia snorted, her eyes sparkling. How could she ever believe she wasn't beautiful?

She was precious to me already.

"What makes you think I crafted this with my very hands?" she asked with a hint of the spunk that would see her well through life.

I tilted my head, my lips twitching upward. "Didn't you?"

"Not the bread. Well, I fried it this morning, but I didn't make it. Veegar did."

"Veegar?"

"He works in the kitchen." A pensive look took over her face. "He helps me when he can."

"Why do you need help?"

"My stepbrother . . ." She shook her head. "It doesn't matter."

"It does to me."

"Eat." Her hand flicked toward the meal. "I'll look at your wounds while you eat if that's all right."

I nodded and dug in, savoring each bite because she'd brought this meal to me.

"It's still warm. It should taste all right too."

"You brought it to me, so it's the best meal I've ever had."

Her pensive expression didn't fade. "You say the sweetest things when you shouldn't."

"You deserve sweet things, sweet talk, Nia."

Ignoring my statement, she gently unwound the bandage from my shoulder and studied the wound, nodding. "You *do* heal fast. Look at that."

The skin had sealed over, and while the scar looked fresh and a bit pink, it felt normal. Shifting it told me it would be almost like new within a day or two.

"I'm going to bind it again if you don't mind," she said.

"Leave it open. The air's good for it. I don't think we need another bandage."

Her upper teeth compressed her lower lip. "If they see you're healed, they'll make you fight."

"I suspect I won't get out of at least one battle before I find a way out of this trap."

"No one ever escapes the compound." Her shoulders lifted with her sigh. "The only way out is if you die."

I cupped her shoulder, gently squeezing. "I'm not going to stay here long enough for that to happen."

"What will you do? Believe me, everyone tries to break free but there isn't anything my stepbrother hasn't seen, hasn't suppressed. I've . . ." Her gaze dropped. "I've helped a few creatures escape, but they didn't need provisions."

"I'll find a way to survive anywhere."

"So you say, but the desert's a harsh place. If you plan

to cross it, you'll need water, food, things that don't just magically appear from the air."

"I'll find a way. Don't worry about me."

"You're so kind. Gentle. I can't stop from worrying."

I sensed she hadn't experienced much in life, and I was going to do all I could to make sure she not only didn't have to worry about me, but that she also escaped her horrible life in this compound.

"You deserve only sweet things in your life," I said as she finished binding my mostly healed wound.

Someone banged on the door. "You need help in there, Nia? He's not threatening you, is he?"

"No!" Panic filled her eyes. "No. He's still unconscious."

"Brunt won't be happy with that. He wants the orc in the arena tonight. Talked it up all over town."

"Brunt's very determined," she said softly, rocking back onto her heels and straightening. "Watch out for him."

I planned to watch out for everyone here, including her, though in a different manner than the rest.

Staring down at me with concern, she worried her lower lip again. "I should go. Finish your meal and pretend you're unconscious. Please."

I nodded, not wanting her to worry.

Footsteps faded in the hall.

I caught her hand as she turned to leave and tugged her to stand between my thighs.

My pendant blazed. My cock started swelling.

All I wanted to do was bury my face in her neck and

breathe in her amazing scent. Kiss her plump lips. Roam my hands across her lush body. She was so tiny that with her standing and me sitting, we were at eye level.

"You, um . . ." Her gaze snapped to my mouth.

"Do you need something, sweet?"

Her lips twitched upward before smoothing. "I keep telling you I'm not sweet."

"To me you are."

Her sigh bled out, and her fingertips teased across my shoulders, stroking. Did she realize she was doing it?

"No one's ever looked at me the way you do." She closed her eyes but for only a moment. "As if you . . . want to eat me up."

I did. So much. "I'm not scaring you, am I?"

"Maybe I should be frightened by the heat in your eyes. With others . . . I don't like it. But your gaze makes me feel things." Her hands fidgeted on her skirt, pinching it and releasing, over and over. "I've survived by making sure I never feel *anything*. With you, I can't seem to hold myself back." Her head tilted, and she frowned as if remembering something. "When others stare at me intently, I cringe. When you do it, I just . . ."

"What?"

"I want to fall into your arms. It's wrong. I know this. You're Brunt's captive. You'll be forced to fight in the arena until you die." Her face tightening, she shook her head. "When I first started healing the creatures my brother brought here to fight, I let them into my heart. But death has a way of stomping through your feelings like a beast rampaging through a delicate flowerbed."

Her fingers tightened on my shoulders, clinging as if she never wanted to let go. "I try to keep my emotions in check, and I've been able to do that until you."

"Mate," I breathed. How had I found this precious person in such a horrible place? She was a delicate flower blooming in the middle of a forest path with a herd of shaydes roaring her way. They'd trample her body. Crush her spirit. Destroy her soul.

It gutted me to think there wasn't anything I could do to prevent it.

Her eyes, swimming with tears, met mine. "You offered me a kiss last night. If you really meant it, I'd like to do it. I . . . haven't willingly kissed anyone yet."

Willingly?

"Who forced this on you?" I growled, peering around as if threats lurked in every corner and I could crush them.

The fear in her eyes made my heart come to a shuddering halt. "It doesn't matter."

"It does to me." I'd kill anyone who hurt her, touched her except with kindness—something I suspected didn't exist in this horrible place.

"Let it go."

How could I?

"If you don't want to kiss me anymore, I understand. I thought . . ." her sigh slipped out, so lonely and sad, "It's silly of me to want to be kissed by someone who actually cares."

"Nia," I breathed, tugging her fully against me. "There isn't anything I want more than to kiss you."

"I'm curious about how you taste, what it feels like to be held by you." Her lips twitched upward again. "And I'm curious to see what tusks feel like against my mouth."

"I hope my kiss means more to you than just satisfying your curiosity," I teased, watching the play of emotions in her eyes. Her face was so open and expressive.

"Kiss me like you want me? Like you never want to let me go." Her voice cratered. "Can you do that? I don't mind if it's just pretend on your part. I want to feel everything. Once, if never again."

"Nia." I wanted to rage through this place, lay waste to whoever might've done so much as look at her with anything but kindness. If I could lift her into my arms and carry her from here forever, I'd do it this instant. But I was as trapped as her, and for now, all we had was this moment. A first for us that might need to last a lifetime.

Her mouth quivered. She was so pretty, so perfect. I couldn't look away. Her kindness and caring made me lose all train of thought, made me forget what I wanted to say or do. She was a force that moved the world and only in her eyes could I find stability and hope.

I wanted to memorize how she looked in this moment, eager and a bit shy, determined yet ready for me to reject her.

Her gaze reflected her growing desire for me.

I could stare at her for the rest of my days, taking in the color of her eyes, the softness of her hair, and the way she looked at me with complete trust. With hope that I could help her escape this place if only for a moment.

How could I ever deny her?

I'd give anything to have one carefree moment with this woman. I felt hopeful yet doomed to love her while never being able to touch her completely.

Escaping this place and taking her with me should be my only goal, yet I needed this moment with her as much as she did. She'd already begun to capture my heart with her sweetness, the gentle way she'd cared for my wounds and my soul.

Need shot through me, and my skin burned. My cock was on fire already, and we'd barely touched.

My hands shook. What if I messed this up? Our first kiss should be everything.

As I drew her close, holding her face, her eyelids fluttered. Her lips parted.

Desire made me careless, reckless even. Ravenous for her. It was all I could do to keep one ear cocked toward the hall. If I lost myself in her like I craved to do, I'd endanger us both. We walked a fine line between a future and death, and I wouldn't do anything to put her at risk.

She looked at me intently, her gaze locked on my mouth, and when she swayed toward me, I couldn't resist.

As I leaned close and breathed in her scent, I stroked the soft skin on her face.

Her eyes shot to meet mine, and heat flared there.

Touching her was going to be my undoing. I'd gone

from seeking ways to escape this trap as soon as possible to planning how I could take her with me while burning the entire place down on the way.

Maybe that's what I needed to do. Rampage through the compound like a beast and leave nothing but waste behind.

I captured her mouth, though gently, when I ached more than anything to plunder. She was an elkern frozen in the woods, and my only goal was to warm her. Shelter her. Show her she'd never again have a reason to be afraid. Such a foolish thought when I couldn't even protect myself.

Kissing her filled my soul with joy.

Deepening the kiss, I held her between my thighs. If she pulled away, I'd release her immediately, but for now, all I could do was drink in the amazing feeling of her mouth beneath mine, her fingers gripping my shoulders as if all she'd ever need in her life was me.

I traced my fingers through her hair, marveling at how soft it was, how the strands reminded me of the finest sinderfluff.

Her mouth opened, and she tentatively touched her tongue against mine. Heat shot to my groin, and my cock throbbed, shouting I needed to fully claim her. Make her mine forever.

She tasted like lindenmint tea, plus pure hope and sunshine. Everything good in life, everything I'd ever crave.

Her moans made me tug her closer. I wanted to devour every bit of her, then go back and do it all over again. Show her how perfect things could be between us, how much I needed and adored her already. She was easy to fall for; incredibly easy to love. She'd be my undoing, and I'd gladly surrender.

Whimpering, she pressed herself against my chest, her fingers flailing and then gripping. I sensed the emotions between us were as new for her as they were for me.

I spanned her waist with my fingers and picked her up; her legs splaying wide to wrap around me. Still, our mouths remained locked together, as if we wouldn't be able to breathe if either of us pulled apart.

Her fingers streaked across my shoulders to the back of my neck, urgent and demanding, before she speared them into my hair, tugging. Her heady sigh told me I had her exactly where she needed to be, and when she sucked on my tongue, my cock nearly exploded.

I was so lost in Nia, in her touch, I'd gone completely out of my mind. There was nothing but her. Me. And this craving neither of us could deny. If only we could remain locked together like this for the rest of our lives.

She rocked against my abs, rubbing herself while guttural moans ripped up her throat.

I turned and laid her on the bed, lifting my mouth from hers. "Mate."

The blaze of my pendant sobered me, reminded me of where we were. Who we were.

And how much danger we still faced.

As much as I wanted to kiss her again, touch her

everywhere—no, give her a bit of joy she could treasure —this wasn't the place or time.

We might never have that place and time.

Need pulsed through me, urged on by my body's primal response to my pendant. I was a rabid beast craving her. One simple touch would complete me.

My damn cock throbbed, telling me to take her now while I could. To claim her. I wanted to show her what we had was pure and good and perfect.

"Not the place," I growled.

Her wide eyes met mine, and she shook her head. Her fingers left my hair to trace across her puffy lips. A look of wonder filled her eyes. "That was . . . I can't describe it, but it was everything I needed." Her lips quirking up was all it took to gut me completely. I was ready to drop to my knees and beg her to smile at me all the time. "I didn't even feel your tusks."

"I think your lips fit between them."

"Yes." Her breath caught, and her brow furrowed. "I guess I got lost there for a moment."

"*I* got lost in *you*." So devastatingly lost.

"Is it always like this?"

"Not for me."

"You've kissed others." I couldn't mistake the wistfulness in her voice.

"Never like this. Never like you." And I wouldn't be with another again. How could I do so when all I'd ever want was her?

Stark terror shot through me. Before I met her, while I lay on my bed wondering if I could make it out of this trap without permanent injury, I'd been willing to try. But now I had so much more than my own life to lose.

The thought of Nia being hurt, of her suffering even one bruise, devastated me, and there was no turning back from that.

It was said that when a clan's pendant chose a mate for an orc, they fell hard and fast, and I was proof that saying was true.

Despite my determination to think only of myself, nothing and no one else mattered but Nia.

I surrendered my heart and my soul to her completely, laying them in her tiny hands.

"Where do we go from here?" she asked.

"We escape this place and make sure we're not recaptured. And then I'll take you wherever you wish to go." It would kill me to tell her goodbye, but how could I make demands when we'd only recently met? She wasn't orc, she wouldn't necessarily fall hard and fast for *me*. "I won't leave you until you feel safe."

"What if I want to stay with you, Dakur? What then?"

"Then I'll hold you close for the rest of my days."

"I think I'd like that. It sounds silly when we just met," her fingertips tapped her chest above her heart. "But it feels right here, deep inside."

And maybe a woman *could* fall as hard and fast as an orc.

Before I made myself climb off this bunk and send her somewhere safe, if such a place existed within the compound, I held her face and stroked her cheeks with my thumbs.

Leaning close, I gently kissed her scars while she quivered beneath me.

This woman should never feel that she wasn't cherished.

CHAPTER 7
NIA

Unable to take my gaze off Dakur, as if losing eye contact would mean I'd lose him as well, I eased open the door to his cell.

I still kept touching my lips, unable to believe how wonderful our kiss had been. He was right; I hadn't felt his tusks. No, all I'd felt was waves of heat washing over me. They both comforted me and made me ache for something I'd never experienced before, something I suspected only Dakur could give me.

My heart hummed, and warmth simmered in my bones as I slipped through the cracked open doorway. I couldn't stop smiling.

When I bumped into someone, I yelped and dropped my basket.

"There you are," Brunt said, his attention slithering past me to where Dakur lay on the bunk, thankfully motionless.

Dakur must've heard my stepbrother, because he groaned and shifted, keeping his eyes closed.

Brunt pushed me aside so hard, I banged into the doorframe. As I stooped down to pick up the herbs I'd spilled, he strode into the cage. Brunt took after my stepfather in height, towering over me, though Dakur had a few heads of height on him. He wasn't bigger either, despite growing up working in the smithy and having the build and musculature to prove it.

He stopped out of the reach of Dakur's chains and lifted his foot to nudge Dakur's side.

I held my breath, hoping Dakur would remain still, that he'd continue the ruse that he was too injured to notice my stepbrother was there. I needed time to put a plan in place, and if Dakur could stay out of the arena, I just might be able to break us both free before he was killed.

"He's healing, but it's going to take time." I rushed over to stand beside my stepbrother, hoping he'd focus on me and not Dakur.

Brunt shoved me aside, and I hit the wall. I couldn't hold back my gasp of pain.

Dakur sprung up to crouch on the bed, his chains jangling and a roar ripping up his throat. "Touch her again, and I will rip your head off."

Brunt retreated back a few steps and shot me a glare. "You said he was still too wounded to fight. He looks pretty healthy to me."

"He . . ." I rubbed my shoulder, knowing I'd have a bruise by the end of the day. "He was. *Is.*" My voice came out shrill. I had to get him away from Dakur. "He really is. Don't put him in the ring. Please!"

Brunt stalked over to me and grabbed the front of my blouse, jerking me up into the air and shaking me. I gaped at him, unable to breathe. Unable to think. My pulse was a herd of panicked elkern scattering across the plain. A predator had found me, and he'd kill me without a thought.

For the first time, I didn't just abhor my stepbrother. I *feared* him.

While Dakur roared and bellowed, straining at his chains, Brunt pushed me against the wall. He spit as he spoke. "Stay out of my way, girl, or you'll regret it. Don't think I won't make good on my threat."

Air jerked out of me as I stared up at him. Horror froze my limbs. I should do something. Anything.

He was going to kill me . . .

Dakur's hand snapped out, and he latched onto Brunt, wrenching him back and forth until he released me. As he hauled Brunt onto the bunk and started punching him, his chains rattling, I dropped to the floor and cringed against the wall, my heart thundering in my throat.

The two males grunted as they flailed on the bed. Dakur landed more blows and kicks before Brunt got the upper hand—but only because Dakur was chained to the wall.

Pinning Dakur to the bed with a meaty hand at his throat, Brunt grabbed a pipe lying on the bed and smacked Dakur in the head.

Dakur slumped on the mattress.

I cried out and raced toward him.

Brunt hauled himself off the bed, rubbing his jaw and twisting his neck and if he needed to put it back into alignment after his run-in with Dakur. He grabbed my arm and hauled me against his body, glaring down at me. "You lied, and you're going to pay."

Tossing the pipe against the wall, he dragged me to the door of the cell and out into the hall. The pipe fell on the floor with a harsh clang and far beyond Dakur's reach, but that was the least of my worries.

As Brunt yanked me toward the stairs, all I could focus on was Dakur lying unmoving on the bed.

CHAPTER 8
DAKUR

My brain swam into focus, then slithered back into what felt like deep mud, over and over. Each time I woke, I remained conscious a bit longer.

Nia. I had to help Nia.

With that thought driving me, I made myself wake up, sit on the side of the bunk, and stare around, hoping to find her here with me.

I was completely alone except for the slow drip of water into the bucket.

"Nia," I croaked, rubbing the big bump on my head. Good thing orc skulls were thick.

I spied my pipe lying near the door and stretched out as far as I could, but I was unable to reach it.

Grunting, I sat on the side of the bed and lifted my pendant. I gently blew across it, over and over, using the tone I'd tested with the water bucket.

Only after what felt like forever did it skitter and clang, sliding closer across the dirt floor. I strained and was able to grab it. Relief flooded me that I was no longer unarmed.

Brunt had used it against me, and I'd hide it, though I doubted he'd forget it was here.

Despite my head pounding, I worked with my pendant, trying new tones, but I couldn't discover any that did more than send a breeze through the cobwebs tenting the corners of my cage.

Using the pipe, I worked on the chains binding me to the wall, struggling to break them free. Worry for Nia consumed me. I kept picturing Brunt hurting her. He'd make good on his threats; that was clear, and the thought of her suffering because of me made me want to rip my lungs from my chest.

A growl kept rising in my throat, but I shoved it back down and focused on loosening the pin imbedded in the stone wall holding my right hand. When it started wiggling, I released a grunt of satisfaction and began working on the one binding my right leg. I'd work all day and night if that's what it took.

Until I was free.

Then I'd go after Nia and, as soon as I tracked Brunt down, he'd feel my wrath.

A subtle scraping sound rang out in the hall, and I stilled. I sat with my back against the wall, covering up the evidence of my efforts, and stretched my legs out in front of me.

As the door clicked, I lowered my eyelids and pretended I was half-unconscious. I should've continued Nia's ploy instead of letting my anger rule. But he'd hurt her, and nothing would stand in my way when it came to protecting my sweet, kind female.

Brunt stepped inside and shut the door carefully behind him. He stomped forward but stopped well beyond my reach.

I let my head loll, though I watched him through slitted eyes, my fingers twitching on the pipe lying along my right thigh—and out of his view.

"Stop pretending," he snarled. "I know you're fine. You're an orc and damn near indestructible. That's why I bought you. You'll make me wealthy before something kills you."

"Where's Nia? What have you done with her?" I barked, my eyes opening fully.

"None of your business." He took one step closer, still remaining beyond my reach.

"If you harmed her, I'll kill you." I assumed I'd have to kill him anyway, but I'd make it sooner and drag out his death for hours if he'd hurt her.

"I don't believe you're in a position to harm a teetser, let alone make threats." A slick grin grew on his face. "I like how you fight, however. It bodes well for the ring." Pivoting, he stalked to the door, tossing over his shoulder, "Your first battle's two nights from now, so prepare yourself."

"You just hit me on the head, and you expect me to battle?"

"No, I expect you to do all you can to stay alive." Turning, he leaned against the closed door. "I imagine you've got a little thing for Nia. A lot of men do, naturally. She's compliant, curvy, and she'll do whatever a man asks under the right hand." He flexed his fists at his side and if I could end his life now, I'd do so.

"I haven't touched her or done anything to her." It was vital I convince him I wasn't interested in her in any way other than as a friend. I suspected he'd hurt her even more if he knew how much she meant to me already, let alone that I'd kissed her, and she'd responded so sweetly. "She bandaged my wounds and nothing else."

"Her behavior suggests she has some fondness for you." His low, grating laugh rang out. "No idea why. You're an orc. She can have almost any man she wants in the village, so why choose you?"

Why indeed? I'd thank the fates that they'd chosen her for me for every day of what appeared to be my very short life.

"What she thinks about you won't matter for long," he said. "In five days, I'm holding an auction and whoever bids the most gets her. I imagine she'll be much too busy with her new husband after that to worry about you."

I snarled, ripping at the chains pinning me to the wall, nearly falling on the floor for my efforts. I may have somewhat loosened them, but the damn things remained deeply imbedded in the wall.

"Touchy, aren't you?" His grin only grew wider. "See? I sensed you had a soft spot for our little Nia already." As quickly as his grin rose, it fell into a deep scowl. "Don't think you'll ever come close to her again. Don't think you'll touch her."

"Nia chooses who she touches."

"In that, you're wrong. As her stepbrother, she's under my control. Everyone in the village would agree. She'll do as she's told."

My growl ripped out. I couldn't hold it back.

Brunt's smile returned. "You really do care for her, don't you? All this uproar because she gave you simple healing, huh? I noticed her puffy lips. Kissed her, didn't you? Well, savor it for as long as you can because it's the only kiss you'll ever get from my stepsister. She's been told to stay away from you. If I catch her here again, you'll both pay."

He turned to leave.

"You want me to fight?" I snapped, struggling for self-control. Where my mate was concerned, I'd do anything, even sacrifice myself to make sure she escaped this nightmare. "Then let's bargain."

Brunt paused with his hand on the knob, not turning my way. "I don't think you have anything to offer me."

"Then you're stupid."

Whirling, he stomped toward me again, but he didn't come close enough for me to grab him and wrap my fingers around his throat or smack him with the pipe. I'd never been a violent orc. My people tried to do all we could to help each other and preserve the world around us and ourselves for future generations.

But right now, I'd kill anyone who threatened Nia.

Brunt gnashed his teeth and lifted his fists. "I'm anything *but* stupid, and you'd better remember it. Who runs this entire show? Who owns the building surrounding you, plus others in town? Who controls Nia?"

I could say something that would make him madder, or I could play this game in a smarter way than him. With everything at stake, I opted for the latter.

"I'll fight in your arena," I said in a reasonable tone despite my urge to snarl.

"Of course you will," he huffed, deflating already. While he was strong, and he'd fought well, he was mostly made up of bluster. "It's fight or die."

"I assume you take bets."

"And I win most of them too." Pride came through in his voice, and I was tempted to stoke it, but there was only so far I could go without being completely disgusted with myself.

"I assume you're shouting out that you've got an orc ready to battle." I got to my feet, not an easy task while chained at four points to the wall. Straightening, I glared down at him, noting how his swallow shuddered along his throat. He was big, no doubt comfortable using his fists more than his brains to make a point. Those beneath him must have a healthy respect for his anger. But if he was like most of his kind, he was greedy. He already said he'd choose coins over what Nia might want for her own life.

"Some know I've got a special surprise for two nights from now," he said slyly. "Few know I bought an orc."

"I was caedos of my clan." When he frowned, I explained. "Leader."

"Bet you fought for that position."

Actually, I inherited it from my father, but that didn't mean I wasn't prepared to fight for the right to rule or that I hadn't trained in case I'd need to. While my clan never battled to the death, we trained from the time we could lift a staff or mace, and with threats coming at us from all around, there wasn't one of us who couldn't defend themselves to the death if need be.

"How many do you think will bet *against* an orc?" I threw out at him.

His face fell. "Not many."

This time, I was the one with the grin. "Then perhaps I should lose my battle in two nights."

"If you lose, you're dead. Think pretty Nia will mourn your loss?"

I ignored the taunt. "Stop the fight before then. Mention something about me fighting wounded, not being at my best. Use some excuse that'll convince everyone you're going to give me another chance once I've healed. I imagine most will put their hard-earned coins on whoever I fight two nights after that, but you'll bet on me."

"*Two* nights?"

"If you say I'm wounded, wouldn't it be kind to allow me to heal enough for the next fight?"

His brow furrowed, and while I'd called him stupid, I didn't believe it. He was crafty, or he wouldn't have gotten this far. "Why would I play this game with you?"

"Because I promise you, I'll win my second round."

"You don't have control over that. No one really does."

I flexed my arms and chest. "You'll have to trust me in this. I can beat anyone and anything you toss into that arena with me or lose just as easy."

"I respect someone who can brag as well as me." His frown deepened, and he tapped his chin, deep in thought. "I could win a lot of coins in both fights if I knew the outcome already."

"*If* I choose to win the second."

His teeth snapped together. "You just said you would."

"Come now. You know there's always a price." In his world, that is. In mine, life and those we loved were the most precious, never coins or wealth.

"I get that. I don't do anything without knowing I'll profit from it myself." Even to the point of selling his stepsister to the highest bidder.

"I'm only going to play this game with you if I get something in exchange."

He stiffened, his hand dropping to his side. "I'm not sharing any of the profit with you."

The last thing I cared about was money. Everything I needed could be obtained by hard work and from the world around me—other than Nia.

She was all that mattered.

"I don't want a share," I said.

"What *do* you want?"

"To be unchained and alone for twenty minutes with Nia."

He snarled. "She's a virgin. I won't let you touch her like that."

I huffed. "I'm not going to fuck her."

"Every other man would."

It was all I could not to sweep out the pipe—assuming I could reach—and hit him. If he fell toward me, I'd lift him up and slam his head against the ceiling, then fling him to the floor.

"I respect her." I said it with everything in my heart, though I doubt he'd hear my true emotion. "I just want to make sure she's all right, that she's unharmed."

"I won't hurt her. That would keep me from fetching a high price for her at the auction."

This male was complete slime, not worth the ground she walked on. "Twenty minutes with her the night after my second battle."

He looked me up and down. "You'll lose two nights from now?"

I nodded.

"Then win a lot for me two nights after that?"

"Exactly."

"Everyone will bid on you the first night." He snapped his chops in glee. "And when you lose the first round, their confidence will be shattered. They won't dare bet on you the second time around, especially when I match you with the most vicious creature known to mankind."

My heart froze. "And what would that be?"

"I've captured a shayde."

CHAPTER 9
NIA

Brunt dumped me in my room, stepped back into the hall, and locked the door behind him.

I banged on it until the skin on the sides of my hands ached and bruises started to form. Then I went over to the only chair in the room, sat, and started plotting.

About an hour later, Brunt returned, unlocking my door. He stepped inside and locked it behind him, depositing the key in his pocket.

After tossing a wrapped bundle on the table by the door, he stomped over to where I sat in a chair beside my bed. I was tempted to rise, but I couldn't do anything he might see as a challenge. Instead, I wrung my hands, hung my head, and did everything I could to look chastened.

He stood panting over me, and a snarl roared up his throat. "Don't think I don't know what you're doing."

I scrambled to my feet and eased around my bed, out of reach of his clenched fists, though that meant I couldn't escape other than by lifting the window and diving through the opening. "I was doing what I always do, healing a wounded person."

"You were touching him!"

Spittle flew, but I held my chin up and met his glare with one of my own. "Be reasonable." It was all I could do to keep my voice emotionless. I wanted to shriek, beg him to tell me Dakur was all right. "I can't heal someone if I don't touch them."

"You *like* the orc, don't you?" He watched me closely, waiting for me to reveal something he could use against me.

I suspected I was halfway in love with Dakur already, but even under torture, I wouldn't tell Brunt that.

"No more than any of the beasts I've healed." I kept my tone calm, as if I was in control of myself and this situation, when I kept fighting the urge to either vomit or sneak through my window and find a way to reach Dakur no matter what it took or who I had to stomp through to get to him. "Is he alive?"

He snorted. "I wouldn't kill an investment."

The tightness in my heart eased, though not by much. This situation was tenuous. One wrong move, and it would fall apart.

"Your mouth looks like he kissed it." His gaze fell on that one area.

I resisted touching it, remembering the wonder of my first kiss—of *Dakur's* kiss.

"I startled him," I said softly, *meekly*. "His hand snapped out, though he didn't hit me hard." It hurt to lie in such a way about Dakur. Our kiss was precious to me, and I'd cling to the feeling when things got worse, which I suspected they would.

"I'm moving up the auction," he snapped.

"No." I rushed to him and took his hand, a gesture that made everything inside me cringe. It was all I could do to sound like a little girl, to make him think I was weak, defenseless, and willing to do whatever he asked. "Please, Brunt. You said I'd have time to get used to the idea." He hadn't exactly said that, but he might not remember. "Let me talk with those who might bid. I'll be sweet and encouraging, and they'll only offer more."

"Why would you do something like that?"

"Don't force me into a horrible situation." Could whatever I stepped into be worse than this? "If I talk with them, I might develop feelings for one of them." The chance of that was zero. "I'll make sure whoever I choose knows he has my favor, and he'll bid high to make sure he wins. Surely whoever wins wants a compliant, eager bride, not a woman who'll fight him at every turn."

A tic thrummed in his temple, and he wrenched his lower jaw around while he thought about my words. "All right. You'll still go to auction in eight days, but I'll put the word out immediately that you want anyone interested in bidding to come speak with you, to *court* you, though some might refuse."

Eight days? How could I get him to set it back to ten?

"Then their chance of winning will be reduced. Ones who are eager for my hand will bid the highest." I'd make no promises, and I wasn't going to allow any of them to do more than look at me, but Brunt didn't need to know that. He was so slimy, he'd assume I'd give out favors, though he knew I'd hold back the final gift of my body.

He grumbled, but I could see he was relenting.

I was playing a dangerous game, but if he expected me to interact with these men, I'd have to be let out of my room. And if Brunt thought I was going to cooperate with the auction, he might give me my full freedom again.

"I promise I'll behave," I added sweetly, though I had no intention of doing any such thing. "I'll do as you ask until the auction."

"All right, ten days," he growled. "But if you misbehave, I'll lock you inside your room and move up the auction."

"What about the creatures who need my care? What about Dakur?"

"*Dakur?*"

What I said now could keep Dakur and me on the treacherous path we walked together or yank us both in different directions.

"I asked his name," I said carefully. "The other creatures don't talk, but he can."

"It doesn't matter. I want you to stay away from *Dakur*. I'm not arguing on this point."

"I need to examine him." I desperately needed to make sure he was all right. "You hit him in the head with a pipe."

"He survived. I was just speaking with him."

I held in any expression of relief. I'd only endanger

him if I let Brunt see how much Dakur was coming to mean to me. "I should still make sure he doesn't have a head injury."

"Stay away." He stalked back to the door. "I'm not bargaining about this, girl."

"Very well." Sedately clasping my hands, I lowered my head, though I watched him through my lashes.

"I want you to attend the arena event two nights from now," he said.

Had a sly look taken over his face? Letting down my guard with Brunt would mean my very life.

He hadn't forced me to sit beside him in the stands since I vomited while watching a match not long after my mother and stepfather died in the fire. The blood . . .

"Why?" I asked politely.

"Just do it." He grabbed the package he'd placed near the door and tossed it my way. It hit my thigh before falling to the floor. It was soft enough, it didn't hurt.

I lifted it. "What's this?"

"Something that'll increase the bets at your auction. One of my men will bring you to me—dressed in this— two nights from now. No excuses." He grimaced. "And no dinner or liquids for you at least five hours before the event. We don't need you throwing up on my paying customers again."

He left, locking the door. I assumed Veegar would unlock it when it was time for me to help prepare the evening meal, but it paid to let Brunt and his men believe I was stuck here until then.

Worry ate through me like a squitt with a pile of

acorns. Was Dakur really alright? The thought of him lying on his bed in pain made my guts twist into a knot.

After stomping around my room for hours, I sat on my bed and lifted the package, unwrapping it to find yet another low-cut gown, this one made of pale blue silk. It would match my eyes and make my white-blonde hair gleam in the whisp lights covering the ceiling of the big open arena, but I couldn't care less about my appearance.

The only person I wanted to look nice for was Dakur.

I tossed it on the chair and laid down on my bed, plotting. I ran scenarios through my mind, but I couldn't come up with much. Escaping alone was a big enough problem, let alone trying to figure out how I'd get Dakur out of his cage to take him with me.

A spark of a plan came to me, and I was trying to look at it from all angles when Veegar came to release me.

"I'm sorry," he said softly, lifting my wrist and attaching a thin metal ring attached to a thin chain clipped to his belt. "Brunt's orders." His face darkened with shame. "I told him you didn't need this, that I'd make sure you didn't get into trouble."

I wanted to believe I could confide in Veegar, that he'd help me if I begged. Sadly, it would be unwise for me to trust anyone.

He led me to the kitchen where I was released but kept under his watchful eye. I dished up big bowls of the meat and potato casserole that I'd prepped that morning. Unhooked from his belt—though with a stern warning not to run—I carried the platters into the dining room, keeping my eyes down as I placed them in the center of the tables.

The men dug in, dishing up huge portions and eating quickly.

Back in the kitchen, I got the ingredients ready for breakfast and prepped what I could.

I remained busy until the last dish was dried and put away and the moon had risen high in the sky.

With a sigh, Veegar looked around at the sparkling kitchen. "Done. I'll take you back to your room."

At my nod, he reattached the chain and led me down the hall. Only when I was inside my room did he release my wrist and hang the chain and "bracelet" on the wall outside my door.

He said nothing as he backed out of my room, though I read sorrow in his eyes.

The lock clicked, leaving me alone.

I sat on my bed, waiting until the world quieted around me. Then, with a sly smile, I used the tool I'd stolen from Brunt's smithy shop years ago to unlock my door.

With a packet of healing supplies tucked under my arm, I shut my door and slunk through the halls, aiming for one particular cage in the basement.

CHAPTER 10
DAKUR

As I blew gently across my pendant, creating a hum so high-pitched, I could barely hear it, the manacle on my left ankle creaked. Unfortunately, it didn't open. But this was progress. I'd given up on trying to work the tethers from the wall. They appeared to be deeply imbedded.

It had taken me hours to discover the right sound. Now I had to keep subtly changing the angle of my wind until the manacle snapped open.

The whisper of footsteps in the hall made me freeze. I dropped my pendant and stretched out on my bed, generating a snore to fool the guards.

"Nice," Nia said softly, her voice bubbling. She shot me a smile that faded too fast, and she shut the door behind her. Pausing, she studied me before the tension dropped from her shoulders. "You're all right," she breathed, her eyes sparkling with tears she quickly brushed away.

"I am. Please don't worry about me."

"I can't help it."

I was so grateful to see her, it was all I could do not to spring to my feet and tug her close. Kiss her. Hold her. Check her over for even a tiny scrape or bruise for which I'd kill her stepbrother.

My chains clicking, I swung my legs over to sit on the side of the bed, ignoring how my head spun and my body ached. Seeing Nia cured whatever ailed me. "It wasn't a convincing snore?"

She sniffed and pushed for a new smile. "If you snore like that, I don't believe I'll want to lie in a bed with you."

My heart flipped over. "And if I don't normally snore like that?"

She walked closer, a packet beneath her arm. "How would you know if you snore or not? You're asleep."

"I *never* snore," I vowed.

Her snort rang out. "That remains to be seen." She sat beside me, lowered her packet onto the floor and looked me over. "Are you sure you're not injured? I had to see you to make sure you're alright."

"I'm fine. Brunt will have to try harder if he hopes to hurt me."

He could, though, and he knew how: by harming Nia.

I cupped her face, taking care not to cause harm with my chains, and tilted her head carefully this way and that, studying not just her physical form but the expression in her eyes. "Did he hurt *you*?"

She shrugged. "No."

It gutted me that I couldn't protect her. "I'll find a way out of this for both of us."

"I might have a plan."

I stroked her cheeks, unwilling to release her yet. She was the light in my cold, dark world and the only reason I found a way to keep existing. If something happened to her . . . I'd rampage through this compound until there was nothing left but smoldering ruins.

"Don't do anything that endangers yourself," I said, though I was well aware I couldn't make demands. Trapped as I was here in this cage and pinned to the wall, I was essentially useless.

"Living here is a risk." She sucked in a breath and released it. "Enough of that. I'm here. You're safe. And I'm going to make sure Brunt didn't leave any lingering wounds." Her hands lifted, but she didn't touch. "Is it all right if I examine you?"

My foolish cock stirred, eager for whatever examination she might be willing to give. "Of course."

Getting onto her knees beside me, she gently probed the welt on my forehead before sliding her fingertips down the back of my neck and to my shoulders. "Tell me if anything hurts."

"Your touch is the sweetest thing." The time for holding back was gone. If I didn't put my heart into my words, she might never know my true feelings. "I live for you, mate. Know this."

"Dakur." Her face pinched. "You say the sweetest things."

I tugged her into my arms, and we tumbled backward, her lying across my chest. "Take what you need from me, mate. I'm here for you always." I'd make sure this remained so.

She pressed her face against my chest, breathing me in, before lifting her head. "I'm not hurting you by lying on you, am I?"

Only my poor cock that ached to be buried inside her.

"Not one bit." My pendant flared, something it would do until we'd completely come together. After that, it would extinguish and never flame again, not until it was passed to a subsequent generation upon my death or as a gift from me. Then it would burn for them when they found the one person they were fated to love for a lifetime.

She straddled me, and her hands continued their journey down my chest and around my waist—which tickled and made me laugh.

"You're not hurt," she said with so much pain, my laughter stilled. Knowing she worried, that she cared, completely undid me.

"I'm not," I wiggled my brow. "Though you're welcome to continue with your examination."

A mischievous look took over her face. "You're sure you're not injured anywhere, that you have no place on your body that needs my attention?"

I grinned, marveling at how amazing she was.

"So many places." If only I could love her completely, show her how much she meant to me, how eager I was to take her from this wretched place. We'd flee to my clan where I could cherish her always.

"I dream about you all the time," I rasped. "Ache for you just as much. You're everything, my sole reason to keep fighting."

"Dakur," she said, climbing up my body to kiss me.

I shifted us around until she was beneath me, a tough task while chained. The thought of being pinned to the wall like a beast made rage growl through me, but it was easily nudged aside by Nia's kiss. She was sweet and innocent and all I'd ever need.

Denying her—denying *us*—would be impossible.

Her kiss was so full of fire, and the way she held my shoulders, as if she never wanted to let go, made my pulse thunder. I threaded my fingers into her hair, holding her head to deepen our kiss, and she parted her lips for me, letting me in. I claimed her mouth like I wanted to claim all of her, teasing my tongue across hers while she bucked her hips up against mine. Her legs wrapped around me, tugging me down greedily, and my groan worked up my throat.

Leaving her mouth, I kissed the line of her jaw while her fingers roamed my chest.

She was all I wanted and nothing I could ever have unless I could find a way to free us. I shouldn't think about that when this moment meant everything, but I couldn't help it. I stroked along her waist to the sweet dip beneath her breasts, and she pushed her chest up.

Her moans of pleasure made me ravenous.

Shifting to the side, I watched her face as I ran the pad of my thumb across her budded nipple.

"Dakur," she gasped, pressing her breast into my

hand. "I need . . ." She shook her head. "I don't know what it is, but I think you're the only one who'll ever be able to give it to me." She lifted her head and claimed my mouth again with reckless abandon. My cock rocked against my loincloth. It would be much too easy to claim her fully, to show her the beauty of our bodies coming together, but this wasn't the place.

And there may never be a right time. Not for us.

I devoured her with desperation, slanting my mouth across hers, trying to infuse everything I had into the touch of my hand on her breast and my lips on hers.

Her fingers slid through my hair, and she tugged gently, drawing me closer until I didn't know where she ended, and I began.

This was so wrong, yet incredibly right. I hated that I could only love her in this wretched place.

Even if I took her here and now, I'd never be fully satisfied, but a longing to live only in this moment spiked through me.

I lifted my head and held her pretty face. "Mate. I wish I had the words to tell you what you mean to me, what knowing you care means."

"I'm falling in love with you, Dakur."

"Nia," I breathed, kissing her again. I couldn't stay away. I'd *never* be able to stay away.

"Show me," she said with a touch of desperation in the grip of her fingers on my shoulders and the way she strained up toward my hand. "Please."

I would never claim her here, but that didn't mean I couldn't show her pleasure.

CHAPTER II
NIA

His gaze locked on mine as he slowly bunched up my skirt, taking it all the way to my waist, exposing me to his view.

Suddenly shy, I wanted to tug it back down, but this was Dakur, the orc I'd long for forever. I had nothing to hide from him.

I was his, and he was mine. Nothing and no one could tear us apart. If Brunt found a way, I'd follow Dakur to the very fates and demand they give him back to me.

His fingertips glided up and down my thigh, making my nerves come alive. Making *me* come alive for the first time in my life. Only this male could make me feel whole.

My skin flushed as heat spiraled through me, centering in my core. I was innocent to a male's touch, but that didn't mean I hadn't found pleasure on my own during the deep, dark night. I knew what he sought, what *I* sought, and I was eager to claim it from him.

With slow, delicious circles, his hands slowly made their way up my thigh to the juncture between.

"Nia," he groaned. "You're so wet, so perfect."

I spread my legs, inviting him in. When he started kissing me again, his mouth feverish on mine, I lost all control. I clung, needing him so much while every nerve ending in my body caught fire.

He kissed down my neck, and my breath caught.

"You're mine," he growled against my hot skin. "All mine forever."

"Yes. Yours." I came alive for the very first time. This might be the only time we could be together. I'd sneak out every night, but one of these days . . .

I didn't want to think about that, not while I had *this*.

He slid my undergarment down and after I'd hitched my legs through it, tossed it aside with a heady groan.

"You are amazing. Utterly perfect," he hissed. His gaze darted up to mine. "All of you, from . . ." Rising up over me, he kissed my forehead. "To this." He traced his lips down the scars on my face. "And to this." He stretched and touched my toes. "There's no one more beautiful, more wonderful than you."

His words sunk into my heart, and for the first time since the fire, I felt beautiful if only in his eyes. His opinion was all I needed. His *heart*.

He freed my breasts from the top of my gown, and his soft groan rang out. "More beauty. More perfection."

My breasts were big, too big most of the time. I hated how they jiggled, how they drew attention. But in

Dakur's eyes, they were beautiful, and that was all that mattered.

When he sucked my nipple into his mouth and swirled his tongue across it, I nearly exploded. My moan jerked out of me, and my pulse roared up into my head.

His fingers stroked between my legs, and my senses spiraled. Warmth and utter, decadent sensuality made my body melt. I surrendered to his touch, to this male who was my everything.

Dakur was the only male I'd never be able to get enough of. No matter what happened, be it the auction and being forced to wed another, I'd carry this moment with me. I'd crave him always, and no one else would ever be able to compare.

I stroked his chest while he rolled my nipple with his mouth.

And when he slid a finger inside me, I growled.

He lifted his head, watching my face while he pumped his finger in and pulled it out. When he added another, the delicious stretch made me gasp. His thumb stroked my clit, and I flamed, bursting into an inferno that threatened to consume us both.

He grinned, flashing the tusks I'd grown to love as much as him. "You're amazing. I love how beautifully you respond to me; how sweet you are. But the night's not over yet."

Sliding lower, he kissed my belly and parted my thighs. As he crawled between them, he grinned and hooked my legs on his shoulders. "Open up for me, love.

Let me taste what I've been craving since the moment I met you."

"You wanted to . . . be between my legs the moment you met me?"

His smile widened, showing off his gorgeous tusks. "I'm a simple male. All I need is you. Me. Us."

When he placed his mouth where his fingers had just been, I gasped with exquisite joy. My heart pounded and whimpers escaped my lips.

My breath hissed out, and I shifted on the bed, overcome by how amazing his tongue felt stroking my clit. "Dakur."

"Yes, mate?" he mumbled against my flesh.

He wanted me to think? No, all I could do was *feel*. His heat and the clever way he used his tongue in a place no male had ever been before.

His tongue stroked from my clit to my entrance, and when he stabbed it inside, his groan of pleasure shot from his chest. He growled as he licked and swirled the scratchy surface across my inner walls.

He looked up and slid his tongue out and up across my clit, giving it a flick that made my eyes roll back in my head. "You taste perfect. So good."

I slid my fingers through his hair and latched onto his horns, holding his face between my legs.

In response, he devoured me, sucking and swirling his incredible tongue around, driving me closer and closer to the crest of something amazing. I sensed when I tumbled down the other side, it would change me forever.

His fingers glided up across the plane of my belly. When he rolled my nipple between his thumb and forefinger, pleasure roared through me.

He sucked on my clit; the hum vibrating through my pelvic bones and heightening the flames licking inside me.

"I've dreamed of being with you like this," he said against my hot flesh. His tongue speared into me before pulling out. "And like this." His hands left my breast to roll my clit, and he plunged his tongue into me over and over, driving my hips up with his other palm as neatly as he drove me through the wonder only he could give.

Heat flared higher inside me, tightening and releasing, each crest shooting me all the way into the sky.

"You taste like joy," he mumbled, his tongue still working me to a fever pitch. "Like hope. Like a spring day full of promise." Looking up, he melded our gazes. "Like you're mine."

I was. I always would be.

With a sharp cry, I shattered, each bit of me soaring out before coming back to nestle within his gentle hands.

AFTER I DRESSED, we laid on his bed, talking of this and that and everything.

"Tell me about your home," I said, trying to imagine being there, of us feeling safe in a place where we could be together forever.

"Ages ago, my clan settled deep within the forest. But

our trees aren't like the spindly ones I saw as I was brought to this compound."

"I can't imagine anything like that. You must stand on the ground and tip your head back, gazing up at them all the time."

His low chuckle rang out. "We don't just look up at them, we move through the canopy itself."

"Among the leaves?"

"Among the leaves."

"It must be amazing up there," I said wistfully. "Gazing down at the ground, watching the birds and squitts play."

"It truly is."

"You said you move through the canopy? How is that possible?"

"First, we have to reach the tops of the trees. We've figured out how to get a teegar, which is a smart plant, to project us up to wooden platforms my clan's ancestors built ages ago. From there, we jump and cross bridges we've constructed, or even swing on vines."

He ran his fingers through my hair, rubbing my scalp, and I moaned with pleasure. It had been so long since anyone cared about me, cared *for* me, that I could barely remember. And it made this time with Dakur taste sweet with a touch of bitterness. Soon, I'd have to leave, and I might never see him again if I couldn't sneak out of my room.

I didn't want to think of the auction, how I might soon belong to another male. How could I lie passively beneath someone from the village when all I could dream about was being in Dakur's arms?

"Did you say plants?" I asked breathlessly. This male barely had to touch me or look at me, and I fell apart.

"We carefully water the plants with diluted fillawate, which is made from a rare fruit that grows deep beneath the ground. The fruit, once fermented, contains properties that make the person drinking it feel happy, but it also gives the teegars the energy they need to assist us."

"And they know that you want them to send you up . . . into the canopy?" I still couldn't quite believe it, and I wondered if I'd ever see such a thing.

It made me sad to think I wouldn't.

He lifted his pendant, and it flared with light, highlighting me lying in his arms, his face full of the same sadness lurking within me, and the chains binding him to the wall. "We use our pendants to communicate with them."

Pendants? This was something else I wanted to learn about.

I could ask him questions forever, and I wanted to learn more about the teegars and his forest, but my time with him was limited. Already, unease scratched across my skin, telling me I should return to my room, that Brunt might find me gone and look for me here. He'd punish us both, but I suspected he'd take most of his anger out on Dakur. Me, he'd marry off tomorrow to the highest bidder.

A shudder ripped through me, and Dakur's arms tightened around me.

"What is it?"

I lifted myself to straddle his waist and brace my palms on his chest. If only I could remain with him always. No, if only we could leave this horrible place and build a new life together. "I need to go."

He gave me a curt nod, though I knew he wasn't upset with me. He must be as worried as I am, if not more. At least I was mostly free to move about within the compound. He was chained to the wall.

"I'll try to come to you again tomorrow night."

In the dimming light of his pendant, I saw a shadow flit across his face, but it was gone so soon, replaced with the curve of a soft smile, that I shrugged it off.

"I've got a plan," he said. "We're going to escape."

"I have a plan too, though it's barely formed."

"Give me a few days to put mine in place."

I nodded and slid off him to sit on the side of the bed.

He joined me, awkwardly trying to put his arms around me with the chains clanking. He somehow cupped my face, his thumbs gently stroking my cheeks.

It wrecked me that he could see past my scars to the real me inside.

"Trust me in this?" he asked, kissing me quickly.

"Always." I leaned into his chest, sucking in his warmth, his spicy scent, and wishing more than anything that I could remain with him forever.

CHAPTER 12
DAKUR

I woke early the next morning and stretched on my bed, switching over to movements that would work my muscles as much as I could while chained.

After my meager breakfast of bread and water, I lifted my pendant and gently blew across it. I didn't make progress with my chains, though the links shifted. I'd find a way to make this work. Somehow.

Brunt showed up late afternoon, standing just inside my cage, glaring. I could tell by the look in his eyes that he was waiting for me to speak first, to challenge him.

Just to irk him, I closed my eyes and pretended to snore.

"Our lovely Nia has dressed in a beautiful gown and is flirting with the first of many men who've arrived to court her," he finally said.

Now *I* felt irked, though I did all I could not to show it. "Good for Nia."

"She'll pick one or two and give them enough of a

taste to make them extra hungry." He leaned against the wall, crossing his arms over his chest. "I'll be curious to see who bids the highest at the auction that I've decided to move up to the evening after your second fight, though my stepsister doesn't know this yet."

Fuck. She was going to cry when she found out.

Giving up my pretense of being bored and half asleep, I swung my legs around to sit on the side of the bed. I lifted my hands. "Care to remove the manacles? We've got an agreement. I promise I'll cooperate." For this moment, anyway. Later? Forget it.

"That doesn't mean I trust you."

"Where do you think I'll go? You could lock my door."

"You might jump a guard bringing you a meal. Nia might find a way to sneak in and show you the way out."

"I only ask for you to remove one wrist manacle and my ankles." Then I could kick if need be, grab someone by the throat—one person in particular.

"No." He pivoted to leave. "I need to go watch over Nia. Play chaperone. Keep the men from taking advantage of her . . . timidness." He glanced over his shoulder, his hawklike gaze locking on me. "She's particularly sweet, wouldn't you say? Her kisses will turn a man's cock into a rod in his pants, and I bet she'll get wet when he tugs on her nipples."

Anger burned through me, and my face grew hot. He was saying this to see what I'd do, to see how protective I was of her. My heart plunged all the way through the floor. I couldn't let him know his words nearly drove me insane.

"Do all men talk about their sisters in such a manner?" I asked blandly.

With anger welting his face, he stomped toward me before stopping out of my reach, his hands clenched at his sides. A few steps closer, and I could grab him by the throat. "*Step*sister. We're not related, though she's still under my control because I'm her only surviving family member."

"I can't imagine she agrees with this."

"You don't know her. I grew up with her." A slick smile grew on her face. "I trained her well."

Also said to irritate me.

With a sigh, I dropped back onto my bed. "Did you come here to malign your *step*sister, or did you have a valid reason for this delightful visit?"

"Just wanted you to know she'll never be yours."

"She belongs to herself."

"That's where she's wrong. She thinks she has some control here, sneaking out of her room at night . . ." He watched me as intently as I watched him. "Coming and going as if no one can see."

I'd have to warn her, but how? It wasn't safe for her to visit me. She had to stay away.

"But I've got eyes everywhere," he said, turning and walking to the door once more. "If she tries to fool me, she'll find out what happens to sweet little women who do bad things."

With that, he left.

I sat up on my bunk again, fretting about where Nia was and if she was safe. Had her brother gone to her to make more demands, or was he letting this game between the three of us play out?

With a low growl, I got to my feet and jogged in place. I stretched again, shifting my muscles through a series of moves I'd learned from a master when I was young and perfected before I was in my late teens.

After, and with a light sweat on my forehead, I sat on my bunk and lifted my pendant. I blew gently across it, hoping I'd hear the click of my ankle manacles releasing.

I DIDN'T SEE Nia again over the next day.

On the evening of my first fight, an older man crowded into my cage with three others. "Up," he barked.

One carrying a chain stomped to me, stopping just out of reach. Two others came over to stand with him, their eyes watching my every move, their long blades trained on me.

"Sit on the side and hold out your hands," the one with the chain said.

"What's happening?" I knew. Darkness had fallen, and it was time to go to the arena.

As for my winning a fight two nights from now, I . . . While I had my suspicions, it never paid to tease the fates, so I wouldn't name it, not even to myself.

"Time to go for a little stroll," the older one said. "You feeling strong tonight, orc?"

"My name's Dakur."

"Name's gonna soon be dead as far as I'm

concerned." The one holding the chain attached it to my manacles, pulling on them until my wrists were locked together in front of my body. "Maybe not tonight, but I hear the boss has something fun planned for you in a few days. Might want to get plenty of rest tonight, *orc*."

"Assuming he survives," another said with a laugh.

I rose to my feet, towering over them, and they had the good sense to back away quickly. "You believe I'll win tonight?"

The old one looked me over. "Orcs are tough."

Not all of us. Some were fragile, though equally cherished. I thought of my mother, blind for many years, yet still the most amazing female I'd ever known. In this compound, she'd be tossed aside. Among orcs, she was treasured.

"I bet you'll win." The old male frowned. "You'd better win. I've put a week's wages on you, and if you let me down . . ."

All I did was return his glare. It wouldn't pay to give away the game now, not if there was even a slight chance Brunt would fulfill his side of the bargain. "Never bet what you're not prepared to lose."

The male growled and leaned close. "Just make sure you win, and I'll bring you something nice for your breakfast."

"More moldy bread?" At this rate, I'd starve to death before dying in the ring.

"Maybe some meat. A slice or two of cheese. I've got an in with the cook, and he'll fix you up a meal that'll rival that of a king's."

That I doubted, but without decent food, I'd get weak. While I didn't expect to be here for more than a few days longer, plans could change. Tonight's competition was still an unknown.

As for the shayde, I had a plan.

"I'll see what I can do," I said as they yanked on the chain, pulling me from the cage and out into a stone hallway. We took a right and walked through an arched doorway and into a second corridor, this one smaller than the first. I ducked down to keep from smacking my head on the dirt and stone mix overhead and shuffled my feet, unable to take a full step with my ankles chained.

I heard the arena before we reached it. At the end of the long corridor, light bloomed, followed by cheers and cries for death.

"I'm not the only one fighting tonight," I said softly.

The old male grunted. "No, but you're the main event, the last battle of the evening." He rubbed his hands together in excitement. "I've gotta go place one more bet before you fight, so don't get too excited, right?"

All I did was swallow hard. I wasn't one who enjoyed delivering death, though I'd do so if it was between my life and theirs. Losing a battle wouldn't be easy, though my pride wouldn't suffer. My worth wasn't determined by a battle like this.

My goal was to avoid dying when I lost.

When we were about ten paces from the arched opening leading to a large, well-lit arena, the one holding my chain stopped and held up his hand. "Let the event ahead of you finish, and we'll bring you out. Crowd's going to love you. Far as I know, no orc has battled here yet, though you might see one or two in the crowd."

"Orcs here?" the old one asked, squinting through the metal gate lining the end of the passage, toward the arena.

I also squinted, studying the ring where I'd fight, taking in the stained sand floor, the high walls surrounding it, and the rows of seating areas above that. It was filled with people who rose to their feet and cheered or jeered, their hands overhead or stabbing toward those fully invested in battle.

Two men wearing metal armor fought with long blades, each slashing out in a blur of silver.

They grunted and one leaped forward, rolling and coming up to a crouch behind the other. His blade shot toward the other, but the male spun, and the two swords crashed together.

"Even match," the old male said, peering at the others. "Who says this will end in a draw?"

One of the two with short blades held up his hand. "I'll take your bet."

They exchanged coins.

The other shook his head. "No draws tonight. Boss's orders for that match. It's to the death or unable to fight, and we know how that turns out." His gaze shot to me, and I read excitement there. "I'm really curious to see how you fight, orc. Will you live up to your reputation or shame any orc out there watching?"

If shame bought me time, I was all right with it.

"It doesn't seem fair that they get to battle with armor and weapons," I said, lifting my hands to remind them I still wore chains. "Who thinks I'll win wearing these?"

The men exchanged heavy glances before the old one spoke. "He's right."

"I'm not giving him my blade," one said, backing away. "He doesn't need a weapon. He's got meaty hands, and everyone knows orcs are indestructible. He'll do just fine."

"Can you imagine trying to take it from him after the fight's finished?" another asked. "He'll get no blade from me either."

The old one scowled. "I've bet a week's wages on him winning. I'm not tossing him out there to face it without some sort of protection."

"It?" I asked, my gaze on the males still fighting. One bled from a slice in his belly, while the other staggered, one hand clutching the side of his head where he also bled.

The one holding my chain released a low chuckle. "Caught that, did you?"

"They released the fighter notice in the afternoon," the old one said. "Everyone in the village has been talking about you. Some came just to watch your show. Never seen . . . one of *them* battle before. Bet he's even stronger than an orc."

"Give me a weapon." I waved to my body, naked of anything other than a loincloth. "I'll . . . figure out how to protect myself without armor." Actually, few orcs fought wearing anything but a loincloth.

"I suppose I could find you a sword or something," the one with the chain said, peering around as if weapons would magically appear before his eyes. He grunted and dragged one of the other men close. "Give him yours."

With a scowl, the male grumbled. His hand tightened on the hilt of his blade. "Why mine?"

"Because you're here. You've got a long knife."

"So do you."

"Do it," the old man said. "Unchain him too."

"When it's time, and he's beyond the gate," the one holding a blade for me said. "Not a moment before that. He'll gut me with it, I tell you."

"Why would he do that? Brunt would punish him for sure."

"Him being punished for hurting a guy sounds great unless you're the one staring down at your guts steaming in the sand."

The old one rolled his eyes. "Just before we shove him through the gate then."

"All right."

Two of the men walked to the fence and held onto it, watching the end of the battle inside the arena.

I waited, wondering who or what I'd face tonight. I'd have to be clever. If I tried to negotiate with whoever I battled, would they avoid killing me?

"Are all fights to the death?" I asked the old male.

"Not always. Costs too much to buy new competitors

if you let them die all the time." He scratched his gray-haired head. "Hard to restrain some of the beasts, however."

"Do you use many in the arena?"

"More often than not. They need to be captured, but they put up less of a stink when we ask them to fight." He gave me a slick smile. "Especially if we starve them."

Most creatures would treat you with respect as long as you did the same. Even the deadliest in the forest around my clan could be managed. Stay away from their territory when they hunted, unless absolutely necessary, and only kill when you had great need. And watch for signs they were going to attack. It was easy enough to find shelter in the canopy.

The battle in the arena ended in a draw with both males lifting their bloody arms overhead and stomping through the sand to the roar of the crowd.

"Well, Brunt must've listened to the crowd because he's letting them leave without killing each other," the old male said. "Maybe he's saving the bloodletting match for the orc and . . ." He sent me a slick smile.

"Get ready," one of the men at the gate said over his shoulder.

The other stomped closer. "Let's take him partway inside and lock the gate. Unchain and arm him after that."

"Good idea," the other said. He yanked me toward the gate while the other unlocked it, then shoved me through the opening. It banged shut behind me.

"Don't get any wild ideas," he snarled as he unlocked

the manacles on my ankles and tugged them away. He reeled back, watching my every move before nudging his head to my wrists. "Lift 'em."

I remained placid and cooperative because I didn't want to risk entering the arena without a weapon. Now wasn't the time to fight the guards.

"And our next competitors are a special surprise," someone shouted inside the arena. "Let's bring the first one out and introduce him, shall we?"

Once free, I flexed my arms and legs and held my hand out for the weapon.

The male glanced at the others before giving it to me with a scowl. "Don't damage it."

I snorted. "I'll protect it with my very life."

The old man reached through the gate to nudge my arm. "Just make sure you win."

Stomps rang out from the fighting field, but I couldn't see past the guards.

"Bring out our new competitor, guys," the person in the arena shouted.

"That's you. Go." Someone shoved me from behind, though I barely moved from their efforts.

Tightening my grip on the long blade, I strode out into the arena. I stopped in the middle and peered around, taking in the stands full of mostly humans, though I spied two orcs frowning down at me.

An elevated box was mounted in the center to give those seated there the best view.

I took in Brunt, and beside him . . .

Nia.

CHAPTER 13
NIA

I hated this snug dress. Hated sitting in the box elevated above the arena.

And I hated Brunt.

But if I'd refused to attend the event, he would've dragged me from the room by my hair and tossed me into a seat even if I was only dressed in my nightgown.

I fidgeted while two males battled in the arena and breathed a sigh of relief when Brunt indicated with a nod that he'd permit a draw. The crowd had called for it, which was why he'd probably relented.

If the rest of the night continued like this fight, I might finish it without throwing up. It hurt to see creatures and people injured. Most of the time, my stepbrother would let me tend to them afterward, but sometimes, he'd make them wait and suffer until morning.

"Why do I have to be here?" I hissed, shooting him a glare during the lull between the finished battle and the next. I was doing all I could to act sweet and compliant, but my nerves were frayed. If this kept up, I'd snap.

In the arena, men smoothed the sand—as if that mattered—and the prior competitors strode toward the arched exit on the right.

"You look lovely tonight, Nia." Brunt gave me a sneer. "Nice to see you wearing the gown I selected. Other men are noticing. They'll bid high. You can count on it."

"You're disgusting." I'd had it. He made one horrifying demand after another, and I was fed up. The sooner I could escape this place, the better. My only wish was to make sure his fighting business fell apart before I left, though I had no idea how I'd do it.

I had no idea how I'd escape, though I refused to give up.

"The mayor's brother is salivating," he said.

Literally salivating down his chin while he gaped at me in my red dress earlier today. I'd pretended to simper, telling him in a lisp that I *so* hoped he'd bid for my hand in marriage. He'd left after telling me he was going to count his coins and borrow what he needed.

"Others will be too," Brunt added. His brow narrowed, though he kept his attention on the arena. "I'm beginning to think I don't want to sell you quite yet, little Nia."

My heart flipped with joy but only for a moment. If he cancelled the auction, he'd do so to arrange something bigger. He might even drag me to the city to auction me off there, and then how would I help Dakur?

"I have time to work on the others," I said stiffly. "We have a deal."

He shrugged and his attention shot to the gate where the next competitor would emerge. "There will be more bidders in the city."

My heart fell even further.

"You can't go back on our deal," I barked.

His slick grin rose again. "I can do whatever I want, pretty Nia, and there's nothing you can do about it."

Tears of frustration rose in my eyes, but I blinked them away, refusing to show him how terrified I was of what he might do next.

I needed to get my plan in place soon and flee—but not until I could make sure Dakur could escape with me. If we were lucky, we could run until we reached his forest. His clan would help us, wouldn't they?

"I want you to watch this match in particular," Brunt snarled, yanking my hands down from my chest and placing them on my lap. "If I catch you closing your eyes or covering your ears, you'll regret it."

Swallowing hard, I gaped up at him.

"You understand?" he said in such a deadly voice, it would freeze water solid.

Helpless, I could only nod.

The announcer talked up the next event, not naming who'd battle.

Silence descended before the announcer yelled. "Bring the first competitor out, guys! It's time for our next battle."

The entrance gate on the left opened, and Dakur strode out with only a long knife in his hand.

He looked up at me and, for one moment, I saw affection in his eyes. But when he turned his gaze to Brunt, his eyes sharpened. He gave me a curt nod before turning to face the other side of the arena.

"What will our orc think of who he's fighting?" Brunt asked slickly.

The right gate opened, and a huge, stony male stomped out holding a club almost as long as I was tall. He stopped in the middle of the arena and looked up at everyone gaping his way before tipping his head back and bellowing.

The stony male turned to face Dakur, and I almost swore he tilted his head, his expression sly. But when he tipped his head back again and snarled, then raced toward Dakur, my heart cringed against my ribcage.

Dakur braced himself as the stone man approached, his blade held by his thigh. Before his opponent could run him over, he dove to the side, rolling and coming up in a crouch.

"His name's Rock," Brunt said out of the side of his mouth, not looking my way. "Strolled right into the village and asked for me by name."

As Rock rushed toward Dakur again, his club swinging, Dakur leaped and tumbled above the stone man's head.

"Why would he want to do something like that?" Terrified I'd soon see Dakur killed, I wanted to look away.

But I couldn't. If he could fight for his life, I could find the will to watch him do it.

"Said he'd heard about my arena." Out of the corner of my eye, I caught Brunt's chest puffing. "I've got a solid reputation for holding the best games."

"I see." I sent him a glare, though it held no kick. I needed to remember to keep my wits about me. Angering him wouldn't make this situation any better.

"He said he wanted to battle, that he was an amazing fighter, and he wanted me to put him up against someone worthy." He shrugged. "I thought your orc fit well enough."

"He's not *my* orc," I said carefully. "I've told you. I just helped him when he was injured."

"Don't bother to lie. You think I can't see your face right now? I know you well enough. You're scared out of your mind that he'll be killed." His attention shot to the sand.

Rock snarled and flung his club at Dakur, hitting him in the chest.

Dakur stumbled backward, slamming into the ground. He lay there for a moment while silence echoed in the arena.

I couldn't help it. My hands clenched; I leaned forward. I couldn't breathe. I could barely think.

"Don't be dead. Don't be dead," I whispered.

Brunt's slick grin rose, and he lifted his voice to mimic mine. "I only cared for him when he was injured, dearest stepbrother. This orc means nothing to me!" His harsh laugh rang out. "Why do you think I moved up the auction?"

"No," I gasped.

"Two nights from now, Nia. Be ready."

"Why?" I wailed, still waiting for Dakur to get up off the sand. The stone man watched him as if he suspected a trap.

"You're getting sweet on the orc, and I won't have it. I've got plans for you that I'm not going to let you interrupt." His hand lifted between us, and he rubbed his fingers against his thumb. "Plans that are going to make me very wealthy."

"You already have enough money."

"There's never enough money."

"Get up," I rasped to Dakur. "Please. Get up." My heart was crushed, and I couldn't look away. Would I lose him in something as horrible as this when I'd only just found him? It wasn't fair. He deserved to live. We deserved a chance to be together.

Rock stomped over to stand above Dakur, panting, before he slammed his fists against his own chest and roared.

Darkness clouded into my vision, followed by a burst of relief when Dakur stirred.

"Looks like our orc doesn't have what it takes," the announcer called out. "I'd call that a loss, wouldn't you, Brunt?"

I looked at my brother, taking in the slick satisfaction on his face. Would he insist Rock kill Dakur?

"If you do it, I'll never forgive you," I bit out, clenching my fingers so tight, my nails gouged my palms. "I mean it. You want me to cooperate with this farce of an auction two nights from now? Then you let Dakur live."

"I'm not heartless," Brunt said with a shrug.

He was. Whatever heart he was born with had long since shriveled.

As Dakur staggered to his feet and wavered, looking as if he'd fall once more, Brunt turned fully my way. "What will you do if I let him live?"

"Anything," I hissed. "Anything!"

"We'll talk about my conditions tomorrow."

"Alright."

Brunt lifted his arm and gave the signal that Dakur could live.

CHAPTER 14
DAKUR

Brunt gave the signal for us to stop fighting. I'd done as we agreed and let the other male defeat me. What Brunt didn't know was what the stone man whispered as he steadied my arm and lifted his other to the approval of the crowd.

"Be ready," he said.

I wasn't sure what he meant, but the look in his eyes suggested I needed to trust him. As did the subtle nod he gave the two orcs sitting in the audience. They then rose and left the arena without looking back.

The only problem was that I wasn't sure I had time to wait for whatever he might have planned. For all I knew, he would fight me again soon, and this was his warning that he'd kill me next time.

But that concerned look in his eyes . . .

I let the guards lead me from the arena, pretending to be more injured than I was. I clutched my head and let them think I hit it when I fell. My poor head sure had taken a beating lately.

I also kept rubbing my chest and made my breathing sound raspy. Maybe they'd believe I had a punctured lung, plus a head injury, and that I was so wounded I wouldn't be able to think about escaping.

I'd be ready in two nights, though. And when I had my time alone with Nia . . . I hid my grin.

It wouldn't be long before we were gone from this place.

After resecuring my manacles, the guards led me back to my room, rechaining me to the wall and leaving me with nothing more than a grumble about getting me something to eat and drink—maybe later. I suspected later meant tomorrow.

I lay on the bed with my pendant lifted, blowing across it over and over without moving the manacles one bit. If I wasn't so desperate to make this work, I'd give up. If it was just me I was fighting for, I'd be sorely tempted.

But Nia was involved. I had to free her from this trap as much as myself.

What did the stone man mean?

Growling, I sat up on the side of the bed, wincing at the pain in my chest, though it wasn't bad. I could breathe easily, which told me nothing was broken. It was almost as if the stone man had put on a show of seriously injuring me while not carrying through. He'd hit me a few times with his club, but the blows had been glancing, not finding full impact. This wasn't what I'd expect from a being bigger and stronger than an orc. He could've killed me with one swipe of his meaty fist.

I laid back down and must've dozed because I woke to the whisper of footsteps in the hall and my door cracking open.

Nia hurried inside with her basket. When I caught her eye, she sobbed and rushed forward, collapsing on her knees beside my bed.

"Nia." I sat up, my chains jangling, and lifted her off the floor, onto my lap.

She cried in my arms. "I was so worried. I thought you were dead. Rock hurt you badly." Her hands roamed my chest. "I shouldn't be crying. I should be examining you. Helping you as best I can."

"I'm fine. Really. Look." I couldn't hide anything from her when I only wore a loincloth.

She ran her fingertips across the center of my chest, her touch so light, it tickled. When I grinned, her watery smile lifted. "You're sure you're not horribly injured and hiding it? You hit your head, too, right? And I saw him hit you with his club multiple times."

I gently wiped her eyes. Tilting her chin, I gave her a lingering kiss, soaking in how wonderful it was just to be with her. To hold her. There was no one who could make me feel the way this woman did. I'd die to protect her, but I'd sacrifice everything just to stand in her light.

"You kiss me like you feel all right," she said, her smile growing stronger. She snuggled against me. "I hated sitting there while you fought. I wanted to find a sword and stand by your side. Defend you like I know you would me."

"Knowing you were relatively safe keeps me going." It was a struggle to maintain hope, to tell myself there was a way out of this for us both. It would be so easy to give in, to fight when told, sleep and eat in between, to sink into the pool of misery I felt growing within me.

Rising onto her knees to reach, she cupped my face and examined it before kissing me again, her tongue sweeping across mine in a way that made my cock stand at attention and my heart thunder. This female. She meant the world to me, and I'd do anything to show her.

Lifting her head, she gave me a full smile. "I'm so grateful you're not injured."

I tumbled her onto the bed in a tangle of limbs and stupid chains I could barely work around to hold her.

Despite our treacherous situation, there was no place I'd rather be. No one I'd rather be with. She was everything to me.

Heat flared through me, making my body ache and my skin overheat. She stroked my arms and stared up at me with complete trust in her eyes. I wasn't sure I deserved that trust, though I'd do my best to prove myself worthy.

"Nia," I groaned.

Undeniable need filled me, and I stroked my fingers down her side. "You're soft. Incredibly lovely. Please know that I'd give all I am to be with you if only for one moment."

"I want you, Dakur. All of you. Everything you can give me."

Need made my heart pound like the thunder of a beast's hooves on the plain, but there was no way I'd stake my love on her body in a place like this. She deserved everything pure and right. Perfect just like her.

Everything I was had become wrapped up in her. Emotions spiraled through me, so much more than simple happiness. She made me feel as if I could conquer the world, tame the wildest creature, and capture the very stars in the heavens. If I could do so, I'd give those sparkling entities to her, and she could string them and wear them as a necklace. They wouldn't outshine her beauty.

I kissed her again, savoring how such her simple touch took me out of this wretched place and into a world spun by the very fates themselves.

My pendant flared, once again telling me she was my fated love, the only person who'd ever complete me.

I lifted my head and made myself remove my hand that had found its way under her blouse to her breast. Her nipple was a hard bud, and I'd kill to be able to suck on it for hours.

I kissed her nose and pressed my forehead gently against hers, staring into her eyes. "You make me want to let everything go and focus solely on you."

"I want to spend hours kissing you, feeling your touch. It's not bad."

"Never," I vowed. "It's perfect like you."

Because I was worried I wouldn't be able to resist her

for much longer, I sat, my infernal chains clinking, and tugged her onto my lap, wrapping my arms around her.

"I've saved money," she said. "I found where the guards hid the keys and stole the one for the manacles. I know that they're apt to drink too much in the evening and fall asleep not long after, remaining asleep through the night. That's why they haven't caught me when I sneak down here. Though they wouldn't put up much of a fuss if they did catch me. I'm in and out of this area so often, healing one creature or another, that they're used to seeing me at all hours." She looked up at me. "My point is, I think we can use this to our advantage." Her fingertip ran along my right wrist manacle. "If we can get these off you, we can escape. I don't know where we'll go, but I'm not afraid to try to cross the desert. We can carry water, food, and . . ." Shadows flitted through her eyes. "I mean, I assume you'll want to escape with me. If not, I want to help you get out of here. All the other creatures, too, if we can. No one should—"

"Mate." When she looked down, I tilted her chin to meet her eyes again. "I love you. I want to be with you for a lifetime." One side of my lips curled up around my tusk. "There's no one I'd rather escape with than you."

She snuggled against my chest. "I don't know what I'd do without you, Dakur. You've come to mean so much to me." Leaning away, she locked her gaze on mine. "I love you too."

"Mate," I whispered, holding her face and kissing her gently. The stars could wink out in the sky. Even the sun could stop blazing. Darkness might try to consume everything around us, but my love for this woman would light up what was left of this world.

Something banged in the hall, and we froze.

Her breath jerked inward as she slid off my lap, her gaze shooting around the cage, seeking a place to hide.

I rose as quietly as I could and tucked her behind me.

But the sound wasn't repeated.

"Maybe it was a chall," she said softly. "Feral ones live down here, hunting creatures smaller than themselves."

"You should go." If she was caught . . .

I didn't want to think about what Brunt would do to her, how I wouldn't be able to stop him from hurting her.

"I'll be fighting again in a few nights," I whispered, turning to hold her in my arms. "I'm going to win and in exchange, your stepbrother has promised to give us twenty minutes alone together and me without these." I lifted my arms, making my chains rattle.

Her breath caught. "I can't believe Brunt agreed to something like that."

"He's greedy."

"There isn't anyone or anything he wouldn't sell." Her eyes lit with hope and excitement. "But this is wonderful. We can escape."

"That's my plan." I needed more than a vague idea for how I'd do it, however. *Had* the stone man been trying to send me a message? I couldn't trust that he was. If we were going to get out of this trap, we'd have to do it without anyone else discovering our plan.

"I'll have things ready, and we'll run," she said.

"Not without taking this entire place down first," I said fiercely. "We're going to destroy it."

"I might have an idea for how we can do that." Her head tilted. "My stepbrother is overconfident. He's become lax. He used to hire guards for all his businesses in town and for the compound, but lately, he only employs those who work here in the cage area. If I could bring you something that would make this compound collapse on itself, could you use something like that?"

"What do you mean?"

"There are all sorts of things in my brother's glass and stonework shops, and it was only by chance that I was there one day when they were experimenting. Brunt's always looking to make money, and he pays some of his men to dream up new ways to do so. That day, they were mixing various crushed stones, perhaps to find a combination that could be used in the construction of buildings."

"Interesting. Tell me more."

"One time, when three of the crushed stones were combined, a puff of smoke and a loud bang erupted. It sent two of the men flying against the wall and blackened their faces." She frowned. "It scared them. It scared me too. But I noted which stones they used, and I stole some once. They're hidden in my room. I'll get them to you."

"Excellent." I had some ideas already.

"If it's that volatile, we need to be very careful when we touch it."

"You're clever, mate."

She grinned. "I am. Well, I try to be. I've had to be to survive growing up with Brunt."

"I don't want you doing anything dangerous." I wouldn't be able to help her. Stuck here, I wouldn't know what was happening or where she was if she got caught.

"I often go to my stepbrother's businesses and watch. I've done it since my mother and his father married. It's common for his men to see me poking about." She wiggled her eyebrows. "I'm curious as well as clever. I'll bring the bags of crushed stone to you, and we can talk about what to do with it after that."

"If we can disarm the guards or make them leave for some reason, we can free the other people and creatures and set things up to destroy this place."

"He may rebuild."

"Then we'll come back again one day and not only demolish what he rebuilds but make sure he can't set it up again."

"I can't imagine how we could do that."

I had a vague idea, but I wouldn't be able to explore it until I was free of this place. There were other orc clans in this area. Once I was home, I'd reach out to them, and they'd help.

"We're going to fix this horrible situation," she said, her voice full of hope.

"We are."

"And then we'll be together."

"Together," I echoed.

She looked up at me with so much happiness that I couldn't resist lifting her and kissing her again. I stroked my fingers through her hair and cupped the back of her head, angling it so I could deepen my kiss.

She moaned and pressed herself against me, her legs going around my torso.

What I wouldn't give to take my mate to my clan where we could finally be together. I lifted my head and grinned at her. I was a silly fool. We should be making plans, not kissing and touching each other, but we couldn't seem to help it.

"You're such a welcome distraction." I didn't want to share how horrible it was inside this cage, not when I knew her situation wasn't any better. Stark desperation kept shooting through me. I wanted to remain hopeful, but I couldn't see a way out of this unless I could break my chains. The best way out was to keep practicing with my pendant.

"All I think of is you." Her smile answered mine, and it hurt my heart to see her in this place.

"You need to leave, my sweet mate." I unhooked her arms and legs and stood, gently setting her on her feet. "Two nights from now, we're going to get out of here." My will alone would make it happen. Giving up wasn't an option.

She stood on her toes and stroked my face. "Stay safe." Her frown chased away her smile. "I know you don't have much control over that, though."

"I'll do my best not to irritate anyone. I have value here despite my loss tonight."

"I'll avoid Brunt and come see you again tomorrow night," she said.

"Don't endanger yourself."

"I'll be careful."

With that, she left. I listened until I couldn't hear her footsteps any longer, grateful when I didn't hear the guard's shouts.

Then I laid on my bunk and lifted my pendant, trying over and over to find the tone that would release my manacles.

The next day, Brunt caught me as I was sneaking out the back kitchen door, heading into the alley behind.

"Going somewhere?" he snarled.

Spooked, I whirled around to face him, pressing for even a touch of a smile without much success.

Two of his men flanked him. Their gazes traveled down my frame as if they planned to bid on me at the auction and were trying to decide how much they could afford. One sneered as he took in my face, though he was new here. The others had become so used to my scars they ignored them.

Or the rest of my body and a chance to be in Brunt's good graces was all that mattered.

"The Sainwirth's new infant is sick." I tipped my head to the basket hooked over my arm. "I'm going to see if I can help."

"You realize I can check this." He held up a finger and

one of the men peeled away, striding down the alley to the main street beyond.

My body tensed, and I rolled my eyes. "Why would I lie about something like this?"

"Let me see." He held out his hand.

I gave him my basket, sighing while he rummaged through my carefully organized packets of herbs. "The baby's sick. I need to go to him."

He tossed the basket on the ground as his man returned, puffing from his run.

"Babe's sick," he said.

Brunt grabbed my arm and drilled me with his gaze. "Don't think of doing anything but tending to the child." He held up his hand. "Mikael will go with you."

Mikael stomped over to loom above me. "I'll make sure she sees to the boy and returns to the compound immediately."

"See that you do." Brunt shot me another glare. "When you get back, I've got an interesting project for you."

"What is it?" I tried to sound pleasant, but nothing was pleasant when it came to Brunt.

"You'll see." Leaving me, he went back inside with his other man while Mikael latched onto my arm.

I wrenched away. "My stepbrother may feel he can grab onto me, but you may not." I snarled up at him. "Not unless you don't want a hangover cure the next time you've overindulged."

Mikael hung his head, his cheeks going red. "Don't be like that, Nia."

"Never act like Brunt." With that, I strode ahead of him out of the alley, turning right. It didn't take long to reach the baby's home, though I paused in the open doorway. "Wait here," I told Mikael.

He grumbled, but one sharp look from me, and he sighed and leaned against the outside of the building. "Don't take long."

"I'll take as long as I need. We're speaking of a child here, Mikael. A baby."

"Yeah, yeah." He kicked a clod of dirt with his boot.

I went inside, shutting the door behind me.

My friend Lara gave me a quick hug and lifted her voice. "Thank you so much for coming. He has a fever! He's been sick all night!" Leaning close, she whispered. "I'll cover for you as long as I can."

"Thank you." We both took a great risk, but I had nowhere else to turn. My friend had always urged me to move out of my stepbrother's compound and in with her, but she and her husband shared the only bedroom in their home with their new infant. How could I impose on them? "I won't be long. My brother sent Mikael with me, but he'll wait a bit before becoming impatient."

"I can handle Mikael," she said with a huff. "Just watch me." Her finger tapped my back. "Go. Don't worry. I can handle this."

"Here." I handed her the healing potions I'd crafted. She'd sell them, and while I made her take a share of the money, if I knew my friend, she'd make sure I received almost all of it.

She set the packets on a nearby table. "You'll be leaving soon."

My eyes stung, and I nodded. "I'll miss you."

"I'll miss you." She embraced me. "But I understand. One day, we'll meet up again and we'll visit."

I wasn't sure how that could happen, but I hoped we did too.

I shifted aside the false bottom of my basket and pulled out the well-wrapped package I'd hidden there, tucking it inside the front of my blouse. It jiggled against my belly as I hurried to her bedroom. I only paused to peek at her newborn son sleeping peacefully in his cradle before easing up the sole window and climbing over the sill. I landed on the soft ground outside and rushed down the street, away from her home.

In no time, I'd reached the edge of the village. I stopped and peered around to make sure I was still alone before jogging along the wispy trail winding through the patches of scruffy grass growing on this side of the desert. The grass gave way to sand peppered with clumps of rocks, and at the third cluster of boulders, I stopped and looked around again.

My pulse roared as if I'd run for hours, and my fingers shook as I scooted to the back side of the rocks. There, I rolled a small boulder to the side and dug into the sand, exposing the metal box I'd buried there a year ago. I'd slowly added to my cache, and the package from inside my blouse joined the others. It wasn't much. Dried food, water purification herbs, a jug, and what few coins I'd saved. Most important, I'd stolen two long cutting knives from the kitchen. I swore Veegar saw me, but if he did, he didn't say a word.

Rocking back on my heels, I stared at the small pile inside the box, wondering if it was enough to survive a trek across the desert. For one person, perhaps. Two? I released a fretful sigh. Probably not, but it was going to have to do. I'd heard the desert to the west of the village was the shortest distance to the other side while the rest of the directions were almost double.

But I'd also heard there was a vast forest to the north. We'd head in that direction, and I hoped we could find shelter and rest in the oasises I'd heard could be found in that direction. Orcs lived near some of them. Would they welcome Dakur or kill him? As for me, I might end up trading this dire situation with Brunt for something even worse. At this point, however, we had no choice.

Only death was worse than what we currently faced.

I secured the box and buried it, covering it again with the boulder, then hurried back to Lana's home and snuck inside. Hearing voices in the front room, I stopped at her door, cracking it open.

"And I told you I'm going to see what's taking her so long," Mikael snarled, glaring down at my friend.

She bristled and huffed. "What is it with you men thinking you have a right to make demands?"

"Exactly," I said, easing out through the door and closing it behind me, Lana's son completely unaware I'd been there. "You're so loud, Mikael. You'll wake the baby, and I just got him to sleep. What were you going to do? Challenge him with your sword?"

He grumbled and hung his head but soon stiffened, shooting me a glare. "You took too long."

I stiffened my spine and stepped between him and my friend. "How long would it take you to diagnose and treat a sick infant?"

"Um . . ."

"Just as I assumed." With a huff, I tightened my grip on my basket and stomped around him, calling over my shoulder to him. "Hurry up. Brunt's got his little project he wants me to take care of." Whatever that might be. "You wouldn't want me telling him you were the reason I took so long returning to the compound, now would you?"

As he strode past me and out onto the cobbled street, I mouthed a thank you to my friend. I didn't like risking her like this, but when Brunt started watching my every move a few months ago, I had no choice. She offered— no, insisted—and I couldn't think of any other way I could sneak away to my hidden cache without getting caught.

Over the past few months, I'd treated her for nausea, sore feet, a stiff back, and now her baby for two illnesses. The villagers must think she'd called a plague here.

I hurried back to the compound, stopping only at the herbalist's shop to replenish my supplies and discreetly add a few things to the hidden compartment in the bottom of my basket. I'd only been able to steal so much from the kitchen. It wouldn't pay for Veegar to see me taking much. While I might be able to trust him, I wasn't confident enough about our friendship to test it.

"You're taking too long," Mikael groused when I exited the shop.

"Hangover," I reminded him as I breezed past him, walking stiffly toward the back door of the compound. Constructed of gray stone blocks, it was such a dark, gloomy place. The only bright spot about it was Dakur and the other creatures I'd tended to.

Once I was locked inside, Mikael took off to join the other men, probably to start drinking to bring on that hangover.

I stopped inside my room to take care of my hidden items and reorganized my basket in case I had need of it, then strode to Brunt's office, knocking softly on the door. Maybe he wouldn't hear me, and I could go to my room and hide until it was time to finish making dinner.

Or find a way to get the crushed stones to Dakur.

"Enter," he called out.

Inside, I kept my face neutral while crossing the cramped space and settling in the hard wooden chair across from his desk. Ages ago, I'd determined he would act kinder if I remained passive and compliant. *Kinder* being a relative term with Brunt.

With my hands clasped on my lap, I sat silently while he finished writing something on the paper in front of him.

Finally, he looked up and grunted. "We caught a unique creature on the edge of the village. It killed three of my men before we could trap it."

My breath caught. While I didn't have friends among his men outside of Kengart and Veegar, calling them friends might be stretching things a bit, that didn't mean I hated them all. Some could be friendly on occasion, and not everyone was slime like my stepbrother. "Who?"

He brushed off my question. "That beast is amazing. It's going to be a real killer in the arena."

"What kind of creature is it?"

"One I'd only heard of before." He stood. "We injured it during capture. You need to fix it so it can fight in the arena tomorrow night." He breezed past me, opening his door again and waving his arm for me to hurry.

Tomorrow night . . . When Dakur was supposed to fight.

"Who?" I gulped and put everything I had into maintaining a neutral expression. "Who will you match it with?"

He chuckled, low and slick.

It was Dakur. What could I do to fix this?

Nothing except do everything I could to make sure we escaped. I'd try to find a way for us to get out of here tonight. We couldn't let him fight against a beast that killed three men while wounded.

"I'll do what I can to help it," I said. "But surely, if it's injured enough to need my attention, it won't be healed enough to fight tomorrow night."

"That thing could kill all of my men even if it lost a leg and they were armed to the teeth and wearing full armor. It was only luck that we caught it." He scowled, his hand on the doorknob. "Come on. Don't sit there all day. I'll take you down there."

After I'd collected my basket, I followed him to the

lower level. He took the hall opposite the one housing Dakur and strode to the end where he kept a double-sized cage.

"Stay back," he snarled, pulling a key from his pocket to unlock the barred door. "One swipe of its claws will rip your arm off."

"How do you expect me to heal it, then?" Truly, if it was that dangerous, I shouldn't enter. Although, while I'd like to think I had more value to my brother than whatever poor beast he'd trapped, that was debatable. A creature who could kill all his men in one battle might be worth more in the arena than me at an auction.

"You'll figure it out," he said. "You always do." He swung the door wide.

Something shifted inside the dark cage.

"Do I get a light?" I asked, timidly stepping forward. Creatures liked me, but that didn't mean I might not one day encounter one who'd rather rip me apart than let me tend to its wounds.

Brunt unhooked a whisp lantern from the wall outside and handed it to me, the small light inside swaying.

"Can you spare me a man to hold it while I take care of the creature's wound?" I asked.

"I lost enough men already. It's chained. Just stay out of its reach."

Then how was I supposed to tend to it? "But—"

"Deal with it, Nia," he roared. Pivoting, he stomped down the hall, stopping at the end to speak with the guards inside the last room.

Well, I could hide in the hall or see what I could do for the poor beast. My heart just wouldn't let me leave without first seeing if there was anything I could do to help it.

I held the lamp near my side and carefully stepped into the cage, shutting the door.

When I lifted the lantern and blew across the whisp to make it blaze, I gasped at what I saw inside the cage.

A lizard-like creature at least five times my size and with glowing red eyes rose from where it crouched on the stone floor. With the chains binding it to the wall behind it, it leaped toward me, its fangs bared and a snarl rising up its throat.

I held myself still, not daring to breathe. It was all I could do not to shriek. Usually, a wounded beast could sense I was only here to help. They might not like having me tend to them, but they tolerated it.

But most of the creatures my stepbrother bought had interacted with humans in the past. Many had experienced some sort of kindness from a human at one point in their lives. They were willing to accept someone who treated them gently.

This was a demon. A feral creature who must live deep within the desert. I doubted it had seen a human before my brother's men tried to grab it.

It hit the end of the chains and snapped back, tumbling to the floor with a heavy growl. While it lay there panting, I noted blood on its front right leg, seeping from a gash almost as long as my forearm.

"Oh, you poor thing," I cooed, stepping forward.

It watched me as I drew closer, though I stopped beyond the reach of its enormous paws.

"I only want to help you," I said softly, my heart pounding on my chest wall so hard, I suspected it would soon break free. After lowering my basket onto the floor, I tentatively stretched my hand toward the beast's snout. Maybe if it sniffed me, it would be able to tell I didn't mean it any harm. Creatures knew things like this on an instinctive level.

Fully prepared for it to snap out its teeth, I braced myself to yank my hand back.

It licked my fingers.

DAKUR

"Bathtime," one of the guards shouted, shoving open my door.

Bathtime? As far as I knew, such a thing could only be done with the bucket of water in my cage that I used for drinking. I'd washed. How could I not? But I hadn't felt clean in forever.

"Brunt's orders," someone else said gruffly as they moved closer in the hall.

The last thing I'd expected Brunt to do was order me a bath. What kind of trick was this?

I rose to my feet. Dismayed by my lack of progress, I dropped my pendant onto my chest.

"A bath?" I asked when the guard named Kengart stepped inside, followed by three others bristling with weapons. They were accompanied by a male I'd seen delivering food a few times. Veegar? That might be his name. "This is new." You'd think they'd feed me if care of my body was something that mattered. Although, starvation tended to make prisoners compliant.

"You stink. Boss's orders," Veegar said stiffly, his gaze shooting toward the other men. His hands twitched at his sides. Why was he nervous?

I stood still as they cautiously approached me. "Why does this matter?"

"The village is holding a consortium and mayors from other villages are here to attend," Veegar said. "They'll be at the fight tomorrow night, and Brunt wants you to look better than you do right now."

Kengart smirked and held up a strip of leather. "Brunt even found you a new loincloth. You're gonna look sharp."

Since I couldn't see any reason to fight this, I stepped away while Kengart released my chains from the wall, though I wasn't up for challenging the other guards. If I behaved, they'd get lax.

Then I might stand a better chance of escaping.

They took me down the hall and around the corner. At the end of this section, they led me inside a large room with a circular stone pool about twice my height across.

Veegar remained in the hall. "I'll see you all later." With that, he left, his hurried footsteps echoing in the big open area.

"Get in the pool," Kengart said, poking my spine with his weapon hard enough to draw blood.

It would be so easy to wrench it from him, spin around, and slash it across his throat.

Patience, I told myself. I had no means of escaping,

and even if I could get out of the compound and find a place to hide in the village while I regrouped, I wouldn't leave Nia behind.

I untied my loincloth and tossed it aside.

"Fuck," one of the guards hissed. "He's freakin' huge!"

"No wonder women fantasize about orcs," the second one whispered. "With that between their legs, an orc could make her shriek a billion times while he rode her for hours."

Kengart rolled his eyes and nudged me with the spear again, urging me up the few steps to the top of the pool. "It's more about what you do with what you've got than the length and girth," he said out of the side of his mouth. "And what you can do with your tongue. Youth." His lips tightened. "It's wasted on the young."

Basically ignoring their comments, I climbed into the cold water and settled on a stone seat, groaning at how amazing it felt despite the chilliness.

A bar of soap dropped in front of me, splashing water in my face.

"Wash. Don't waste time," Kengart said. "Brunt may have ordered this, but we don't have all day to babysit you while you lounge around."

I grumbled but how could I complain when I could get clean for the first time in weeks? After I was captured and while they were transporting me to the village market, they kept me in a cage. My only "bathing" came from one of the males throwing a couple of buckets of river water at me and that was before we reached the desert. With my head injury, however, my memory was murky. I seem to remember them dunking me in a pool while we crossed the desert. An oasis? Must've been.

And someone washed me not long after I arrived. I believe that was Nia, though I hadn't asked.

I scrubbed everywhere and washed my hair, rinsing it with a dunk. Then, while they continued to grumble about the size of an orc's cock and whether mine was special or just average, I lounged against the back of the tub, finally feeling like my old orcish self.

"Done?" Kengart asked, poking me in the shoulder with his spear—not breaking the skin this time, thankfully. "Get out. Dry off. Dress." He dangled the new loincloth.

I did as he asked and remained placid while they took me back to my room. Someone had replaced my hay-stuffed mattress while I was gone and left a covered tray that I assumed held another hunk of bread, perhaps this time supplementing it with a chunk of moldy cheese. What a treat.

"To what do I owe this honor?" I asked sarcastically.

"No idea," was all Kengart said, his gaze darting to the other males who'd continued to discuss orc cocks in general. "Brunt sometimes pampers the fighters who win, but we know that's not you." His laugh shook his rounded belly, and the others joined in. "It's probably a mistake, so don't expect prime treatment like this again."

"Your fighters will last longer if you feed them, house them in better quarters. A blanket would be nice. Meat and vegetables. A piece of fruit every now and then.

Healthy people are stronger and can battle longer in the ring."

Kengart huffed while the males resecured my chains to the wall. "I'll be sure to note your comments and deliver them to Brunt."

"This place won't be here for long," I added. "You should find new employment."

The other men left the cage, but Kengart lingered. "As if you'd know how to run an establishment like this."

I scoffed at the term "establishment."

"Orcs are strong and it's not from paltry meals like that." I flicked my finger to the covered food I'd eat, though I'd take no enjoyment in the spoiled goods. "If your fighters are weak, they won't survive."

He frowned, and I suspected my words were finally sinking in. "I'll think about it."

"I assume as head of the guard; you have some say in things like this."

His hands on his hips and his face lightening, he rocked on his heels, eating up my simple praise. "I do, of course. I've worked here for three years. *My* fighters win more than the others' challengers."

"With the right treatment, your fighters could win more often, and I imagine there would be a raise in that for you, let alone more money if you bet on your own crew. Brunt must notice when your creatures and people lose."

"Yeah." He spit on the floor. "You lost the other night. I thought you orcs were indestructible."

"We are when we're well taken care of." I lifted my

hands, making my chains clink. "When we have enough freedom to exercise and train properly. If you leave us tied to the wall all the time, we weaken. You have access to the bathing pool. If your fighters could regularly wash, their wounds would heal faster. And soaking in a tub is great for relaxing muscles." Not when it was cold water, but that wasn't the point.

He strolled to the door. "I'll think about it."

And I'd be gone before he came to any conclusions, but it was worth mentioning. If I could obtain more food, I could hide some for our escape.

"One day, Brunt might not be in charge," I said as Kengart turned the doorknob.

His hand froze, but he didn't turn. "What does that mean?"

I shrugged. "This place doesn't always have to be run in this manner. Someone who, say, paid fighters to battle instead of forcing them might find ways to make a solid profit."

Turning, he scowled. "I don't know what you're suggesting."

"Nothing nefarious. But Brunt's older than you, isn't he?"

"About my age, actually. What of it?"

"Maybe he'll sell or perhaps his hard ways will catch up to him." Someone—like me—might kill him. "Whoever took over could make changes. You could turn this into a more profitable business."

"It already makes a nice profit."

For Brunt. I doubted the men working for him shared

in the spoils. "What I'm saying is that you could build an arena on the surface. Hire men—or even orcs if you pay well enough—to fight for you because they share in the proceeds."

His scowl deepened. "Sounds like a loss if I'm paying them."

"House people right, feed them food that makes them strong, train them, and give them a share, they'll do their best in the ring."

He directed his stare to the floor. "Interesting notion."

"A business like that would be respected." I doubted this one was.

"We do have to keep what we do here . . . somewhat secret."

"I doubt the mayor would enjoy hearing how people and creatures are captured, chained to walls, then tossed into a fight where they more often die than win."

He stiffened. "If you think you're going to tell him something like that, don't even consider it. You're not going anywhere, let alone speaking with the mayors who are coming."

And yet they were attending the show tomorrow night where I would be matched with a shayde.

"What happens if I win tomorrow night?" I asked. "Will I be permitted to speak with Brunt's guests?"

He shook his head. "You really have the nerve, don't you? First telling me how this place should be run. Then teasing me with notions of how I could turn it into a less shady business. Now you're suggesting you'll be part of any party that might take place after the event." With a sigh of disgust, he turned back to the door, opening it. As he stepped out into the hall, he spoke over his shoulder. "Make sure you win tomorrow night, but don't count on going to a party. If you don't win, Brunt has orders."

"What's that?" I called out as he started to yank the door shut.

Pausing, he grimaced. "Just win. Trust me in that. You don't want to know what he'll do to you if you don't." He closed the door and his footsteps faded in the hall.

I stared at the tray. Because I needed whatever nutrition the rotten food might give me, I tugged it onto my lap and lifted the cover.

I gaped down at the plate holding fresh vegetables, fine grains with what looked like a delicate sauce, and a big slab of meat.

NIA

I washed and treated the creature's wounds, marveling that such a ferocious beast could be sweet and tame with me. After patting him a while and making sure he not only had food but clean water, I left. The guards stared at me in amazement as I walked past them, my basket hooked on my arm, but I hid my smile. I'd made a new friend, and I was going to make sure he got out of this trap with us.

Returning to my room, I took advantage of no one watching and tugged the bags of crushed stones from beneath my bed. I stared at them for a long while, wondering how best to transport them, plus how they might be used in our escape.

I carefully loaded them into a large basket, adding small empty bags. Slipping from my room, I hurried back to the lower level and hid the basket in a storage room, way in the back.

Then I returned to my room and bathed, dressing in

my kitchen blouse and skirt. I scowled at the note Brunt left near the red gown hanging by my bed telling me to be ready to entertain more prospective husbands after dinner.

After helping Veegar in the kitchen, I donned the red gown, combed my hair, and spent the evening chatting with the visiting mayors while Brunt watched with a brooding gaze. He'd cleared a front room in the compound and made Veegar decorate it for the occasion. As if a few frills could make this trap look like something fancy.

"Some of them are going to bid," Brunt told me after as he took me to my room. "You did well. They're all salivating about claiming you as their own." Outside my room, he stopped and gripped my upper arm tight, before releasing me. "Don't mess this up."

Wincing, I rubbed the sore spot, but I refused to cry—something I ached to do almost all the time. Brunt would only take advantage of what he called weakness.

He might not see it, but I had a core of steel. A few tears only made me stronger.

"You'll attend the game tomorrow night," he said. "No excuses. Wear the blue dress and be prepared to flirt with the mayors again. After . . ."

"What?"

"Nothing."

I didn't like the hint of secrets in his eyes.

"Very well." Again, it was important he think I was cooperating with this. The thought of watching another match, one I suspected would feature Dakur and the creature, gutted me. But what could I do? There would be no refusing Brunt. If I tried, he wasn't above dressing me himself and dragging me by the hair to the event.

I stepped into my room and after the lock turned behind me, I braced the chair under it and set up my triggers. I washed in my attached bathroom, something Brunt installed not long after he moved me into the compound after the fire. He hadn't added the bathroom for my comfort. If he locked me inside, I couldn't get to the facilities, and he didn't want me "wandering" there late at night in case I came upon one of his men.

Dropping onto my bed still fully dressed, I waited him out. He'd drank a lot during the party, and I worried it would make him angry. He might return to storm around my room and yell. My situation was getting more tenuous by the minute. I wasn't sure how much longer I could remain here before I broke.

To keep from letting worry consume me, I daydreamed about me and Dakur escaping. We'd go to his clan where he'd show me the wonders of his world. His people would accept me. They wouldn't mock my scars, and I'd not only have friends, but I'd also have a husband who adored me.

Grumbling, I sat up on the bed. Dreaming was foolish because none of it was going to come true if we couldn't escape. I'd be lucky if I had some say in who I married. As for someone adoring me, I doubted I'd find that among the males who'd bid on me at the auction.

I rose and prepared to sneak through the building to

visit Dakur. Maybe we could release his chains and run tonight.

If not, just seeing him would cheer me up. Maybe he'd kiss me again. Touch me.

With the heat of anticipation swirling through my body, I teased at the lock. It didn't open, but I kept trying.

When it still didn't release, I stood back, staring at the handle. It slowly turned.

My lungs froze, and I gulped, backing away from the panel with my hands lifted.

The panel shot open, the door and my bells jangling, and Brunt stood outside in the hall, leering. "Going somewhere, stepsister?"

"I was hungry," I said defensively. "I was just going to the kitchen for a snack."

He stomped inside, advancing on me so fast, I could only yelp. Holding my arm, he yanked me back and forth hard enough my head flopped. "You snuck out last night and went to that orc."

"He was injured. If you treat your creatures and fighters like dirt, they'll die before they reach the arena."

"You don't tell me how to run this business," he snarled, spittle flying.

I wanted to call him a fool, to scorn him. But I was close to escaping, and if I did anything to tip him off, he'd make sure I never got away. It wasn't just my own safety, but also Dakur's. "I'm sorry. I didn't mean it. You know me." It was all I could do to force a smile. "I can't help it when it comes to creatures and . . ." This would gut me to say, but I had to. "The orc is a creature just like the others, isn't he? He just doesn't have fur or scales."

Brunt watched my expression, but I kept it blank. "Yes . . . He is. Stay away from him." He pushed me and stalked out of the room, locking it again.

As the moon rose and slunk across the top of the upper level of the compound, I waited. Then I waited some more. When I tested the door, my tool worked.

But one of Brunt's men stood in the hallway, leaning against the wall on the other side.

"Back in your room, Nia," he grumbled.

I gulped, my eyes stinging.

He huffed. "There'll be no slinking around the compound for you."

WITH MY EYES aching from crying, I helped Veegar in the kitchen the next morning. When I finished, I went to my room, washed, and changed into a clean skirt and blouse. I lifted my chin and grabbed my basket.

My stepbrother was not going to keep me away from Dakur.

A guard followed me down to the lower level and waited while I tended to each of the wounded creatures.

When I stopped at Dakur's cage and looked back, the guard stood in the opening to the guard's room, calling out to the others. I hurried to the storage room, grabbed the bag, and returned to Dakur's cage, slipping inside.

I froze when I found his bunk empty.

My heart plunged down to my toes. Had they killed him last night? If he'd fought and died in the arena I'd know, right? I sagged against the wall, breathing much too fast.

"He's not here," Veegar said from the hall behind me. His hands gripped the handle of a cart I'd prepared for the guards. Veegar had added a bunch of things to it, saying he was going to give the guards a special treat today. That was Veegar, though. Often surprisingly generous. "Dakur's bathing."

I blinked. "Bathing?"

He nudged his head to his left. "You know. The pool. He's alone because the guards . . ." His intent gaze slipped to the empty cart before meeting mine.

Laughter rang out from the guard's break room. They were feasting and . . . Veegar had set this up. But why?

"I didn't tell you any of this," he said gruffly.

"Thank you." I waited until he'd clattered the cart down the hall and slid the bag of crushed stones beneath Dakur's bed. Then I snuck toward the pool. When Kengart passed me at a half-run, heading to the break room, I just nodded. He barely looked my way.

If I was lucky, the guards would feast for a while.

I continued down the hall and turned the corner, hurrying to the room on the end. No one stood guard, but I found the door locked. Of course, and I hadn't brought my tool.

A glance overhead revealed a panel in the ceiling. If I remembered correctly, this small passage traveled parallel to the hallway, though I wasn't sure what the purpose of the passages could be. I doubted Brunt even knew they existed. I only did because one time, a chall hid among the supplies in the kitchen. It leaped and scrambled through a small hole in the ceiling, and I stood on a chair to see if I could coax the creature back down. A panel like the one above me shifted to the side at my touch, and I climbed up into the tight space, crawling through it, trying to lure the chall to me with a bit of meat. I'd captured the chall and put it outside where it scampered away.

After that, I looked around as I traveled through the compound, finding more panels just like it in the ceiling and a series of very narrow passages up above. Small channels led in all sorts of directions, though I hadn't had time to explore many of them.

I'd dragged myself through a few of the passages whenever I thought I might not be heard or seen, finding a rickety ladder at the end of one of them that led to long channels on this level. I hadn't explored after that.

Since none appeared to lead outside, I'd basically forgotten about them.

Until now.

Clinging to narrow gaps in the stone wall, I climbed until I could bump aside the panel.

Soon, I lay on my belly inside and slid the section back into place. I moved forward, dragging myself through areas where I could barely fit until I was confident I was above the bathing room. I shifted another panel to the side and was greeted with the earthy smell of water and the sound of splashes below.

After hanging my legs over the opening, I dropped down carefully, landing squarely on my feet.

Dakur sat in the pool, his back to me.

"Time to get out, Kengart?" he grumbled. "And I was just savoring the joy of being clean once more."

"It's me," I whispered, hurrying forward.

He stood up and turned, his eyes widening when he saw me approaching.

I stared at his big cock, so thick and long. It was as beautiful as the rest of him.

CHAPTER 18
DAKUR

"You shouldn't be here, love," I told Nia, quicky grabbing the drying cloth and wrapping it around my waist as I rushed out of the pool. I had to get her out of here before the guards returned.

"I couldn't escape from my room last night. The guards are busy right now. We have a few moments."

That eased my anxiety but only a fraction.

"Brunt had my room guarded and someone kept checking to make sure I was there, so I couldn't use . . ." She waved to a hole in the ceiling.

I stepped closer, looking up. "Where does that go?"

"All through the compound."

We could escape.

"But," she held up her hand, "it's too narrow for you. I can barely drag myself through the passages."

I huffed out a sigh.

She rubbed a red mark on her arm that looked like . . .

"What's that?" I growled, stalking closer to her. I

gently tugged away her hand and leaned forward, examining the area. "Who. Hurt. You?"

"It's nothing," she said, her voice flighty. "I . . . banged it on my bed."

"Brunt." I didn't need confirmation. I *knew*. I gnashed my tusks and peered around as if Brunt might step from the shadows and hold still for my punch.

Her chin lifted and her steely gaze met mine. She was so tiny yet fierce, as if she could take on a pack of ashenclaws and defeat them all on her own. "He's not going to do it again. I won't let him."

"You're right. He's not. We're getting out of here." I dressed in the clean loincloth Kengart left and took her hand, urging her toward the door.

"We won't be able to escape," she cried. "The guards will soon be done with their breakfast. They'll capture you before we make it halfway up the stairs. And Brunt's office is up there. He must be inside by now. He rarely shuts his door. He likes to know what's going on everywhere."

If we found a way to get out of the compound, Brunt would never stop looking for us. This wasn't just about us escaping him. He'd see this as losing a battle. He didn't only want to sell Nia; he had an overwhelming need to always win.

Only my death and her sold for a very good price would satisfy him, and that would only keep him sated until he discovered the next challenge.

"I'm not leaving you here to be harmed by him any longer." Pulling her close, I held her, trying to show her with my arms and the furious beat of my heart that I'd do anything to keep her safe. But we were both aware of how tenuous this situation was, how neither of us was in control of anything.

"We're going to run tonight," she whispered. "I've hidden supplies near the desert, and we'll grab them and go. If we keep moving, we'll get ahead of Brunt and his men."

"How long does it take to cross the desert?"

"Weeks."

Dry heat. Little water. Few supplies. It sounded insurmountable, but I'd tackled worse things in my life. Staying here wasn't an option.

"We'll travel north," she whispered. "In the village, I heard the desert gives way to an enormous forest. Do you think we'll find your clan there?"

I nodded. "After I was captured, we traveled south, so perhaps." If we could escape the compound and make it across the desert to any forest, at least there, we'd stand a chance of survival. We could make our way to my clan if it wasn't near.

"We'll need weapons," I said. Because Brunt wouldn't give me up, let alone Nia, easily. He'd come after us with many men, and I couldn't do this if I didn't have a way to defend her. We'd have to be clever if we hoped to evade recapture. There was also the chance he'd kill me on the spot.

It was better than remaining here.

"I might be able to steal some," she said. "I took kitchen knives and hid them with my cache."

"Don't get caught."

"I'll be careful. I'm allowed into certain areas, and sometimes, the guards are careless and leave blades behind. If nothing else, the kitchen's well-stocked with knives. I'll grab more and be ready."

She took so many risks, and there wasn't any way I could help her.

"I'm fighting again in the ring tonight," I said.

"I suspected you were. Brunt told me I have to attend again. He enjoys taunting me, watching as I struggle to keep a smooth face. I'm terrified you'll be hurt."

"We made a deal. I purposefully lost the last match because we knew everyone would bet on an orc. I'm going to win tonight when everyone will believe I'll lose again."

"It's a clever idea. Brunt loves making money," she said dryly.

Hence, selling his stepsister to the highest bidder.

"When he leaves us alone and me without chains, we'll run."

"He won't follow through on the deal he made with you." She growled. "I know him. He'll agree to almost anything but then renege on it."

"Then we'll escape a different way," I said with a smile. "I believe I've found a way to release the chains."

"How?"

"I'm still working on it, but by tonight . . ." Plans were flying through my brain. We could make this work. "I'll fight and make sure he doesn't go back on our deal. Be prepared to flee when he brings you to me."

"I will," she said with the first smile I'd seen in too long. "We're going to get out of here." She sounded almost giddy; a feeling mirrored inside me. I tempered it. There was too much to do before then to get excited yet, but soon . . .

I hustled her toward the opening in the ceiling, marveling at how she'd not only discovered something I'd missed but traveled through the ceiling. "As much as I want to hold you and kiss you, you need to leave." The guards wouldn't leave me alone for much longer.

"I'll sneak back to my room and be on my best behavior," she said. "Brunt won't suspect a thing."

Footsteps rang out in the hall, followed by one of the guards calling out to another.

Nia froze, her terrified gaze meeting mine.

One boost, and she was up in the ceiling. She looked down at me one last time before sliding the panel back into place.

The guards entered the bathing chamber and secured my manacles, leading me back to my room where they locked me inside.

"Get ready for tonight," one of them snarled. "Although, maybe don't get ready, since I'm betting the beast is going to eat you."

I just stared at them blankly as they secured me to the wall in my cage. I didn't relax until they'd left and locked the door behind them.

That's when a panel in the ceiling and near the door slid to the side and Nia peeked down at me. "All clear?"

"You should keep going," I groaned. "Return to your room and hide."

"I will once I've said goodbye." She shifted around, her body scraping against the passage above, and carefully lowered herself to drop to the floor.

Then she sauntered toward me, a heady smile on her face. "Ohe kiss, and I promise I'll leave."

I would never be able to resist this woman.

Because I wanted to hold her, I tugged her close and wrapped my arms around her. She looked up at me sweetly.

Was it wrong of me to kiss her, to press her against the wall beside my bed, to lift her so she could wrap her legs around me?

I kissed down her neck, savoring how amazing she smelled, how she moaned at my simple touch.

"I want you, Dakur," she said. "I have from the moment I met you."

"I'm yours," I vowed, tugging down her blouse to kiss across the tops of her breasts.

"I mean I want everything." Her fingertips were feverish on my shoulders. She clung to me as if she never wanted to let go.

I lifted my head, studying her beautiful face, the heat and love glowing in her eyes. "Are you sure?"

With a smile, she nodded. "Make me yours, Dakur." Her fingertip flicked my pendant that was blazing once more, reflecting the devotion in my heart for this tiny, perfect woman. "Let's extinguish this light forever."

CHAPTER 19
NIA

"We don't have time," he growled against my throat. "Someone could walk in at any moment."

"We have now. They just chained you to the wall. They won't return until it's time to take you to the arena." I stared at him starkly. "This may be the only time we'll have together."

I could tell he was giving in. He craved me as much as I did him, and we didn't know if our plan would work. This could be the last time we would be close. If we didn't escape, I'd soon find myself with whoever bid the highest at the auction. If I hadn't experienced true love with Dakur, I wasn't sure how I'd be able to stand being with another.

Cradling my head, he kissed me. "You're perfect. Amazing," he growled against my neck. "I'm not good enough for you."

"You're all I need. All I want." My eyes stung with

tears because I was afraid this one moment was all we'd ever have. I wanted to make it last, to treasure each second.

"All I can see is you, Nia. You. Always."

"Always," I echoed. I'd claim what I could from now and hold it close. If we were lucky, we'd escape tomorrow night and someday reach his clan.

Then our new life in safety and love could begin.

Bracing my bottom with one hand, he stroked down my cheek with the other. "I want to make this special for you. You deserve that. We shouldn't do this here. I told myself I wouldn't, no matter what. This is a special time for us. We should be in a pretty meadow, high in the trees, or on a bed of flowers."

"You, Dakur. *You* make this special. I don't need anything but you."

His fingers stroked down my neck and to my breast that he cupped through the thin fabric of my blouse.

"You're beautiful," he rasped, his words sinking into me like the sweetest caress. "Utterly perfect. Utterly mine."

"Yours," I said with a nod, a shiver hitching down my spine.

His mouth claimed mine again, and his kiss seared through me. His mouth still on me, he backed to his bed, sitting with me on his lap.

I straddled him, completely lost in the warmth of his hand on my breast, his mouth demanding on mine. It wasn't hard to put aside where we were, the danger we were in. All I could think of was him.

His chains jangling, he turned to gently lay me on his bed and lifted his head, breaking our kiss.

I keened, needing him, needing more.

His gaze met mine, so intense and pure. "You're mine, pretty one. My mate, my heart, my very soul."

"Yours," I breathed.

He eased my blouse up and over my head, revealing my breasts.

"Perfect," he growled as he devoured first one nipple then the other, bringing them both to hard peeks. I ached for his touch, for what would come next. I knew it would be as amazing as the male in my arms.

While I was already falling apart, he kissed down across my belly, stopping only when he reached the top of my skirt. He looked up at me with so much need, it made my lungs come to a halt.

"Tell me to stop now." His body shook with the intensity of his emotions.

That same feeling was reflected in me. "I can't." My voice was a guttural cry in the room, muted only by the low hum of the whisp light.

"I don't want to hear you can't, because that doesn't imply consent," he growled. "I want you. So much. But you have to want this as much as me or I'm going to stop."

"I'm yours, Dakur. Claim me completely. I want this."

His head cocked; his hooded gaze locked on mine for a long moment before he gave me a jerky nod.

His mouth returned to mine, determined and desper-ate, and I soon writhed beneath him, overcome with emotions I'd never experienced before. His tongue stroked mine while his arms caged me, his body heavy yet heady on top of mine, his knee thrusting between my thighs to part me.

I soon lost track of anything but him, and when his hand bunched my skirt, lifting it up my thighs, I bucked up against him.

Cool air coasted across my naked skin as he tugged my skirt down and tossed it aside, my undergarment following. I was a hot mess, and only he could make all this wonderful once more.

"My perfect mate," he growled as his tongue circled my belly button as he kissed lower. The chains were cool against my feverish skin, and they clinked when he moved, but even that couldn't slow us down.

He urged my thighs apart farther and crawled between them, looking up at me with so much love it made my breath catch.

Then his mouth dropped to my core.

The air jerked out of me as he used his tongue and fingers. Pleasure shot through me, and I spread myself wider, savoring how incredible this male made me feel.

My cry of joy echoed around us.

He lifted his head, grinning. "You like this."

"The fates, yeah." I weaved my fingers into his hair, tugging him back between my legs." Don't stop now!"

"As my mate demands," he said against my flesh. "So I'll deliver."

He licked me and focused on my clit, flicking his tongue across it while my cries ripped out of me. I was so lost in him that the compound could collapse around us, and I wouldn't lift my head and look around until he'd finished what he'd started. I knew he could give me pleasure; he'd done so before.

And I craved what he'd soon do for me now.

"You taste wonderful," he growled, spreading me wider. His tongue stabbed inside me, plunging over and over while his fingers rolled my clit.

I was going to explode. Soar all the way to the moon. Collapse in this male's arms and beg him to do this again.

Could he make this wonderful feeling last forever?

Heat burned through me as I lost myself in the movement of his tongue and fingers. My body shook. I was rising all the way to the clouds, and nothing was going to hold me down.

While he continued driving me ever higher, his other hand stroked my breast, his fingertips tugging on the nipple. I was so far gone, I'd never be found, and I gave into the heady feeling.

When my legs started quaking and I hovered on the cusp, he lifted himself up, his hands bracing on either side of my shoulders, his gaze locked on mine.

"Mate," he growled, seating the head of his cock at my opening.

"Mate." I wrapped my legs around him, urging him closer.

With a roll of his hips, he pushed forward, stretching me with his girth and his need.

I gasped, and he stilled.

"Too much?"

When he started to withdraw, I gripped his arms tight. "No. Now, Dakur. Take me now."

"Mate." His voice was so sweet and gentle. "I don't want to hurt you. I'm big. Too big for your tiny body."

"Take me," I growled, my fingers biting into his arms.

He studied my face for a moment before nodding once more. Then his fingers trailed across my belly, and he seated something on my clit. It started to suck, and I remembered seeing what looked like a smaller cock above the first back in the bathhouse.

While the sensual pleasure of it made gasps erupt from my throat, he thrust forward again, partly seating himself inside me.

The stretch was almost unbearable, and sharp pain stabbed through me, but it was followed by intense pleasure.

"You're with me, mate?" he huffed out, his lungs heaving and his body shaking from restraint.

I stroked his arms where I'd pinched tight. "All the way, Dakur. All the way."

He pushed forward with another shift of his hips, slowly stabbing deeper.

The pressure was so intense, I wasn't sure my body could stretch to take much more, but I needed to feel all of him, *know* all of him.

At the jerk of my head, he eased back and shoved forward again. Two more times until I felt the head of his cock butt against my deepest inner wall.

"Now show me what only you can give me," I said in

desperation. "Claim my body as you've already claimed my heart and my soul."

"You're utter perfection," he said, his body trembling. He pulled out and pushed back inside, the stroke of his cock making flames lick across my bones.

"That's you, Dakur. You." Using my heels on his ass as leverage, I hitched my hips up to meet his next thrust.

His low growl rang out.

At my urging, he started moving faster, driving hard and deep, making my body coil tight and release, over and over. Each time I tightened, I thought I'd shatter, but then he drove me even higher, riding my pleasure as he rode me.

My core throbbed, and I sensed I was going to fly all the way to the moon and beyond. It would be sweet. Amazing. Unlike anything I'd experienced before.

His pendant blazed, highlighting the intense love on his face, making all of him glow like he had become one with the stars.

I cried out in joy with each of his thrusts, whimpering at how wonderful it felt, how much I needed this and him.

He shifted his hips to hit a deeper place inside me, and I felt my inner walls gush.

His groan echoed with mine. "You feel so good, mate. So good."

While his second cock sucked on my clit, nubs on the sides of his main cock quivered, the feeling sinking all the way into my bones.

It was all I could do to hold on. I didn't want this to

end. I needed this feeling to roar through me for the rest of my days.

His pendant flared again, remaining lit as he moved even faster, each shift of his hips forward taking me along the heady ride with him.

I started to shatter, tremors erupting from deep within my core and spreading all the way to my fingers and toes.

"Yes," he groaned, his hips jerking forward, his second cock vibrating faster against my clit. He rode me through that orgasm and brought me to the next.

Only when I'd collapsed beneath him did he give in, throwing himself into a frenzy that made my body surrender once more.

With a groan, he let loose, shuddering as he came along with me.

And that's when the inner light in his pendant winked out.

CHAPTER 20
DAKUR

My body was completely sated for the first time in my life, I smoothed her clothing back into place and laid on my bed, holding her in my arms as tightly as I could while still chained. She was my mate. My love. My only one.

"You need to go," I finally said. Now that I'd been with her, all I could focus on was her safety. It was foolish of me to give in, but given the chance, I'd do so again. I'd never be able to resist her. "I need to know that you're safe."

She nodded and sighed. "I wish we had more time, that we weren't trapped in this compound, that you weren't chained to a wall." She looked up at me with tears shimmering in her eyes. "I wish you didn't have to fight."

"I will protect myself. I would never do anything less. But I don't like causing others harm. This is wrong, and we're going to make it right."

"I hope we can." The discouragement in her voice made my insides clench. It was hard not to feel like I'd never be able to make a difference. But there was a way, and I'd find it.

Holding her gently and with my infernal chains clinking, I sat on the side of the bed. She snuggled in my lap until I urged her to stand. I straightened her clothing, teasing her skin while I did it. When we'd finished, she was breathless, her pupils were blown, and she was moaning, leaning into my arms.

It would be so easy to love her once more, but we were on borrowed time already. Instead, I kissed her deeply, drinking from her mouth while she clung to my shoulders.

I could barely reach, but I was able to give her a boost up through the exposed hole in the ceiling.

She poked her head down, giving me a smile I'd cherish forever. "I put the bags of crushed stone under your bed. Don't mix them together unless you want to feel a big bang. I included small, very sheer bags. Maybe we can fill them and . . ." She shrugged. "Throw them? I'm not sure what."

"I'll think of a way we can use them. Thank you."

"Love you, Dakur."

"Love you, Nia."

I watched as she slid the piece of wood back into place and listened as she shifted her body through the passage to the hallway beyond. If only I could stand guard over her, make sure she left this level and got back to her room without anyone causing her harm.

When things remained quiet, I settled on my bed. The scent of our lovemaking lingered, and I drank it in, wishing I still held her in my arms.

Soon, mate. Very soon, we'll be together always.

I had to hold onto that thought.

I lifted my pendant, practicing once more. This time, I was able to unlock my wrist manacles. I couldn't get the same tone to unlock my ankles, but I was making progress.

With a grin, I sat on the side of the bunk, flexing my arms and shoulders. I rose to my feet and jogged in place, working my lower limbs as best I could while my ankles remained restrained.

When I was breathing fast and felt I'd gotten a decent workout, I sat once more and lifted the pendant, trying again to release my ankles—without success. Frustration drizzled down my temple in a trickle of sweat. The tone should be the same. Why wasn't it working?

When footsteps echoed in the hall, I quickly secured my wrist manacles and braced my palms on my thighs, watching the door. It unlocked, and Veegar poked his head in, looking around as if he expected to find someone with me.

Did he know Nia was here? If so, we'd have to be extra careful.

He stepped in and softly eased the door shut behind him, hurrying forward with a sack in his hand. Pausing just out of reach, he tossed it toward me.

I caught it, holding the bulky thing on my lap. "What's this?"

He glanced over his shoulder and spoke in such a low voice I barely heard him. "You'll need it." He spun on his heel and fled the room, his light steps shifting away quickly.

I opened the bag and sucked in a breath when I found fresh bread, cheese, meat, and pieces of fruit inside, plus a flask of cool water. I ate quickly, finishing it all, wishing Veegar was here so I could thank him.

Dropping back onto my bunk, I grinned at the last items I'd discovered in the bottom of the bag.

Leg sheaths and incredibly sharp blades.

Exactly the protection my mate and I would need for a journey across the desert.

I'd barely replaced the panel in my bedroom ceiling when Brunt unlocked and slammed through the door, dislodging my traps. He glared at them, kicking the bowl. It hit the wall and clattered on the floor. "Where were you?"

A chill scraped across my skin, and I hugged my waist and lifted my chin.

"What do you mean?" I asked. When I should be lying on my bed and dreaming of the wonderful time with Dakur, I was dealing with my stepbrother instead. "You need to leave." I waved regally toward the door. "I need to help Veegar finish preparing the feast you requested for the mayors and dress in the red gown. If you don't leave, I might not have enough time to get ready."

"Where were you?" he blasted.

I took a step backward, my body tightening in preparation to run. If I scooted around him, I could bolt through the halls. Find a place to hide until his wrath was spent.

"I was down in the lower level treating the beast with the injured front leg." Actually, I needed to check on the poor creature again to make sure the treatment I'd given it yesterday was working. "Isn't that what you want me doing?"

"I looked there." His hand snapped out, latching onto my arm, and he shook me. "Where were you?"

It was all I could do to remain calm, to meet his eyes. "After that, I was chatting with one of the mayors."

"Which one?" he asked in that deadly voice I'd come to dread.

"I can't remember his name. I've talked with so many." I said it breezily. Would he believe me?

"I didn't see you in the living area with any of them."

"We took a walk, though we didn't go far. I thought you wanted me to sweet talk them so they'd bid higher." Pray I was far from here before his auction was due to take place.

His gaze narrowed on my face. "If I hear you were with that orc, I'll get even."

I had no doubt about that. "Why would I visit Dakur?"

"Because you want him. I can see it in your eyes."

Because he treated me with respect and love, concepts my stepbrother couldn't fathom.

"I really need to go." I waved to the simple skirt and blouse I still wore. "Veegar needs me."

He snarled. "Make sure you're ready for the games

tonight." A conniving look took over his face. "I've got a surprise for you."

"I assume Dakur's fighting again. You'd take pleasure in watching him lose, I guess." His ego was incredibly fragile. If Dakur showed strength, Brunt took that as a direct challenge. The thing is, my stepbrother was a formidable fighter himself. If he challenged Dakur, my love would have a tough battle ahead.

"Yes, the orc is fighting again." Releasing my arm, he backed to lean against the open doorframe. "But that's not the only surprise."

"Do you plan to throw me into the ring with him?" I was pretty much joking.

He scowled before his face cleared. "That's not a bad idea."

"Then you must be planning to have Dakur battle another person, not a creature. You wouldn't want a beast to rip me apart instead." I didn't know how I found the strength to keep from crumpling at the thought of a beast tearing into Dakur, but I'd lived in this compound long enough that I'd formed a hard outer shell. Now, I hid inside it, quivering with fear I knew better than to show. "Who'd want me if I was covered with even more scars?" I boldly met his glare, teasing my fingertip down the burn scars on my face and neck.

"I guess you're right," he grumbled, turning. "I won't put you into the arena with the beast." He slammed the door shut behind him.

I remained where I was, wondering what else my stepbrother had in store for Dakur and me tonight.

I WENT to the kitchen and helped Veegar finish preparing the meal, a dish made with sand snake—a delicacy in the village—plus tubers picked along the shore of the oasis. We bought those from a woman who stopped by every few days with various goods. We planned a grain dish with the meal. Village farmers grew the grains themselves in the flat open areas near enough to the oasis they could use the water for irrigation.

"Why don't I pick some julippe berries near the oasis and make a cobbler for dessert?" I asked. I did want to pick berries. Everyone loved their sweet tang. But I also had more food I'd stolen from the kitchen I could hide in my cache.

"That's a great idea." Veegar gave me a level gaze, and it lingered as if he was seeking something in my face I needed to keep hidden.

I gave him a sweet smile, relying on the same demeanor I used with Brunt. Act placid and compliant, and everyone left me alone.

"Why not take this with you?" he finally said, opening a lower cupboard and pulling out a coarse sack.

I took it and things inside shifted. "What is it?"

His gaze shot to the door leading from the kitchen to the dining area where Brunt currently entertained the mayors with drinks and light snacks. The door eased open a pinch, and I froze. Would Brunt storm into the room and make me join them? I wasn't dressed for entertaining, but that had never stopped him before.

"My joints are aching," Veegar complained, rubbing his spine and wincing.

"I can make you a tea."

"You're so kind, Nia. I'll welcome the tea. But since I'm so sore, could you please drop that package off with Woolink?"

Unsure who he meant because I didn't know a Woolink, I frowned.

He lifted his hand before I could question him. "Last home at the end of the road leading out into the desert. There's a big outcropping of rocks not far past his house. You know the one." He wiggled his eyebrows.

My belly flipped over. My cache was hidden within that outcropping of rocks. Did he know about it?

As if he heard my thoughts, he gave me a subtle nod. "Go along with you. Hurry to deliver the bag and pick the fruit. Then get back here and start making the dessert. Don't dally. The cobbler needs to be done baking before the mayors and Brunt finish eating the main meal."

"All right." Unsure what he meant but grateful he hadn't mentioned my cache, I scooted out the back door and snatched up the pouch I'd hidden in the alley outside the kitchen on my way.

Three streets down, I slunk into an alley and after looking around and making sure no one was near or watching, I released the tie at the top of the sack and opened it wide, peeking inside.

"Well," I gasped, taking in the wrapped grain cakes, the smoked haunch of meat, small sacks of salted nuts, dried fruit, and empty flasks. A small pouch of water purification herbs accompanied the provisions as well as a sheer thermal cloth that would serve as a decent covering during the nights when the sun disappeared and a frigid wind took over. "This . . ." My eyes stung with tears. This wasn't for a fictious Woolink but for me.

Veegar must know of my plans. If he was trying to help, he wouldn't tell Brunt.

With my hope renewed, I left the alley and hurried through town, stopping as I always did at the last empty building—no Woolink in sight—before darting across the vast open area between the edge of the village and the big pile of rocks. Around the backside, I stooped down and added Veegar's sack and my small pouch to the growing pile in the metal box.

I sat back on my heels and studied the contents. Was it enough? I might be able to steal more food from the kitchen and hide it outside.

If not, it would have to do because we were out of time.

After picking berries and returning to the compound, I made the cobbler and served the meal to my stepbrother and his guests—evading groping hands with a dull smile on my face. All the while, I smiled inside.

Because soon, I'd be able to flee this place forever.

We washed and put away the dishes.

"Thank you," I said softly.

He grunted and rubbed my shoulder.

With tears in my eyes, I returned to my room to get ready for the evening show.

As I dressed, I scowled at the red gown. It draped low,

barely covering my nipples, and silver lace flounced around the neckline, the three-quarter sleeves, and the hem that I worried I'd snag on something and trip over.

But making sure Brunt didn't become suspicious was worth wearing such a hideous dress.

I slipped my feet into the sturdiest shoes I owned, ones I believed I could run in, yet Brunt would accept, and I packed a bag with everything I owned of value. It wasn't much. Everything I'd loved of my mother's had burned in the fire. After stuffing the bag under my bed, I sat on a chair to wait for someone to come escort me to the arena.

Promptly before eight, Kengart knocked on the door, poking his head inside. His gaze scanned the room.

"Are you ready to go?" he asked.

"Yes." I followed him out into the hall, closing my door behind me.

He led me through the halls and down the stairs.

"Do you enjoy working for my stepbrother?" I asked.

He scowled my way. "Why ask that?"

"It's just a question. I'm curious." I kept my voice sweet and pleasant. "Brunt can be . . . snarly, I guess." Mean, actually, but I'd start there.

"What's with all of you asking things like this?" He paused in the hall, gnashing his teeth.

"I'm only me. I don't know who else you're speaking about." I lifted my eyebrows. "Who else has brought this up?"

"No one," he snapped. "Are we going to continue or are we going to stand here all night and talk? If we don't get you there before the games begin, Brunt will rip my head off."

I huffed and started walking again. "As I said, snarly."

"He's under a lot of pressure." He caught up and walked with me. "We all are."

"He makes a lot of money. He has staff who run everything for him. I don't believe pressure explains why he's so nasty all the time."

"You're just angry he's going to auction you off. If you'd picked from the available suitors, you wouldn't be in this position."

I snarled, stopping again. "As far as I know, there were no suitors for my hand in marriage."

He stared toward the tunnel leading to the arena's entrance. Stairs on the right would take us up to the box where I'd sit with Brunt and the mayors.

His face darkened. "You just weren't looking hard enough."

Yuck. Please tell me Kengart wasn't going to bid on me too.

"I don't want to get married," I said, moving forward once more.

"You don't have a say in it, and I'm sure you'll be happy with whoever pays the most. Most women would be thrilled to think men would try to outbid each other to own her."

"Why would any woman want men to compete to *own* her?" I snapped.

"Because it shows she's wanted."

I was already wanted—by Dakur. There was no one else for me, but I couldn't say that.

"Are we going to just stand here or are we going to the box?" I grumbled, using his own words.

He rolled his eyes and took my arm, urging me the rest of the way down the hall and up the stairs.

"As for *him*," he said softly before we reached the top. "Yeah, he's snarly. Too much, most of the time. But he's the boss and there's no other way to look at it despite *some* people spinning dreams about a different sort of place."

Who else had talked to Kengart about Brunt? I supposed it didn't matter. Nothing was going to change, and he'd better get used to it.

As for me, I still had hope in my heart that I'd escape this trap with Dakur.

After nodding and dimpling a sweet smile to the mayors seated in Brunt's box, under my stepbrother's hawk-like gaze, I settled in my usual seat to Brunt's right.

The crowd shuffled and chattered around us, and bloodlust and excitement tainted the air. Bets were feverishly taking place, and many drank ale or ate, gnawing on hunks of roasted meat speared on wooden spikes.

My belly rolled, and I swallowed hard to keep everything down. I'd barely eaten at dinner, knowing how being in this place made my guts churn.

"Are you ready?" Brunt asked with a slick grin. "The show's about to start, and I know you're going to enjoy it. Do remember to keep watching." His fingers pinched the tender skin on my forearm. "No closing your eyes and missing out on the best parts."

"I do as I'm told," I bit out.

"Now there's the lovely Nia I hope to see smiling at the auction tonight."

My chest coiled into a tight ball. "Tonight?" I gulped. "The auction isn't for a few more days."

His hand remained on my arm, his fingers wrapping around it as if he suspected I'd bolt. "I moved it up. My new friends are impatient."

"You promised," I whimpered.

A few people sitting nearby looked our way before returning their attention to their food or the still empty arena.

"I made no promises." His pleasant gaze remained trained on the sandy floor. "I allowed you to please yourself by speaking with potential bidders, but I never vowed not to change the date of the auction."

I couldn't do it. I *wouldn't* do it!

"Please, no, Brunt." It was all I could do not to yank on my hair and wail. How could he do this to me? Our plan was only loosely in place. Would we be able to escape before Brunt sprung his final trap? If he got me inside the locked room with the bidders, I wouldn't leave until I was shackled to my new "husband".

Panic spiked through me, and my body shook.

"You've got a bit of time to get used to the idea," he said. His eyes lit up, and he pointed to the gate on the far right of the arena. "Look. The first and most exciting event is about to get started."

The gate glided open, and a lull fell over the crowd.

Then a beast hurled itself through the opening. It was the creature I'd treated, the one with the injured front leg. It raced across the sand as if it had never had a wound, and I was grateful to see it appeared to be healing.

Coming to a halt, it sent sand flying from its enormous claws. Its glowing red eyes scanned the crowd, and in the silent shock that had followed its entrance, its low growl rang out.

"I'd say this beast will make a fine challenge for *Dakur*, don't you, stepsister?"

Its scaled hide gleamed in the lights, and its tail jerked back and forth in agitation. With bunched muscles, it looked poised to scale the metal fence between it and the spectators or rush back through the gate.

The gate banged shut, leaving it trapped in the central arena.

It released a sharp chitter, its red gaze sweeping the stands for a way out, but there was none.

Then the gate on the left side opened and someone was shoved out. I'd recognize Dakur's hair, his height, and his horns anywhere.

"He has no weapon," I said with a gasp. "And he's chained. How do you expect him to fight?"

Brunt grinned. "I'm sure he'll find a way. Your orc is quite resourceful, don't you think?" From the sharp look in his eyes, he was either testing me to see what I'd reveal, or he already knew everything.

Was I followed when I went to the desert?

"Keep your eyes open, lovely stepsister." Brunt rubbed his hands with glee. "It's going to be amazing to watch the shayde rip your orc apart."

CHAPTER 22
DAKUR

As the guards shoved me through the gate and out into the sandy arena, the crowd roared, rising to their feet in an excited mass.

Someone poked a spear into my back, and I stumbled forward again, barely catching myself before falling to my knees.

The chains around my ankles tangled together and for one moment, I thought I'd faceplant to the audience's jeers. Not that I cared about what they thought of me, but if I wanted to survive the night, I needed to figure a way out of this latest trap quickly.

How did they expect me to battle without a weapon and with my ankles and wrists chained?

A snarl to my left sent me spinning, and my eyes widened to see a shayde leaping against the fence surrounding the arena. The humans sitting behind the metal structure reeled back, some scrambling over the backs of their seats and fleeing to higher ground.

Brunt sat beside Nia. She fretted; her gaze locked on me while a slick smile rose on his face.

I knew right then that he was not going to fulfill our agreement even if I won my fight. He wanted me to die here in the arena.

And he wanted Nia to see it.

"Watch out," she cried, her eyes flicking to her right.

Shaydes were the predators of the forest, and this one would be as vicious as the rest. I'd lifted my pendant, prepared to release a sound that might repel it when it dropped down from the fence and spun to face me.

Taen.

It was all I could do not to call out his name. He was one of the three shaydes I'd found as kits after their mother was killed by hunters. I'd raised them as pets. They loved me.

An amazing plan dropped into my mind. In that moment, I knew exactly how Nia and I were going to escape. The small sacks I'd packed earlier and tied inside the back of my loincloth would only make my plan work better.

I bit back my grin and lifted my chained arms overhead, bellowing out a challenge for the shayde but actually making it for the entertainment of the crowd.

Taen knew exactly why I yelled like this, and he responded as always, tipping his head back to release the eerie chitter that would make prey bolt through the forest in complete terror. He bunched his muscles and sprang in my direction. Each jump was the length of an orc or more. Sand skittered from his claws, and he bared his fangs as if he was going to rip me apart.

As I stood stoically, pretending I'd given up or might leap to the side when the beast reached me, I spied those in the crowd furiously exchanging bets. None would place their money on me, and they'd all be wrong.

I sent Nia a look of reassurance, but I couldn't tell if she received it.

"Dakur." Nia wailed as Taen made the final jump, his claws extended and his scales bristling across his hide. His ruby-red eyes locked on mine as he hit me, knocking me backward to the gasps and cries of the audience. They roared to their feet as I grabbed Taen's neck, straining to hold his head away from my throat.

Nia was on her feet, as was the rest of the audience. Brunt nodded and grinned with complete satisfaction. Tears streamed down Nia's face, and I wished I could reassure her. But for this ruse to work, I had to make it seem as if my death was imminent, that I'd soon be only mangled pieces of orc steaming in the sand.

I kicked up with both chained feet, impacting with Taen's pale brown belly, knocking him to the side. He fell on the sand, and I rolled with him, coming up to loom over him, my chained hands locked at his throat.

Flailing, he sent me flying backward. I landed hard on my back and lay there a moment, the wind stunned out of me.

Taen chittered again and sprung to his feet. As I sat up and scrambled backward with him stalking me, the crowd jeered. They bellowed for my blood, calling me a coward, though it was clear I had no weapons to defeat such a vicious creature.

"Dakur," Nia cried again.

Soon, mate. Soon.

This time, when Taen leaped toward me, I tumbled to my right, putting distance between us. I rose to a crouch as he jumped up onto the metal surrounding the arena, making it clang and those behind it cringe in complete fear.

I lifted my pendant. If there was ever a time for this to work, it was now.

My gaze met Nia's, and I tried to show her I was all right, though I couldn't tell if she saw it. She'd pressed her hands against her throat, and her face was filled with so much sadness it made me want to rip out my heart and hand it to her.

Now, mate. Be prepared.

I subtly blew across my pendant, and the manacles on my wrists fell away, dropping to the sand with almost no sound.

Until the crowd went utterly silent, watching.

While Brunt snarled, I blew again, this time closing my eyes and crafting the perfect tone, one slightly different from the one I'd just created.

The manacles on my ankles released and fell away.

Yessss.

Taen chittered and stalked toward me, exactly like he would if we were at home in the forest.

I scooped up the chains and hurtled them toward Brunt. They hit the metal caging and dropped to the sand with a clang. I hadn't expected them to reach him, but it gave me endless satisfaction to see terror rising in his dark eyes.

Nia's eyes gleaming with tears, she shook her head.

As Taen jumped, planning to tumble me to the ground for more play, I stepped to the side. He swept past, and I leaped, landing squarely on his back. He paused and looked back at me with complete joy. I didn't know how he'd ended up here, but I was grateful to see him.

I pulled the sacks of crushed stone from the back of my loincloth.

With a nudge of my heels, Taen bounded across the sand, approaching the tall metal barrier separating the central part of the arena and the box where Brunt sat.

I leaned forward and whispered in Taen's ear that flickered back before sharpening, pointing forward.

He leaped and soared up and over the mesh metal wall, landing squarely in the aisle to the right of the box.

As Taen stalked toward Brunt, he reeled backward, falling and knocking over some of his guests who wailed in horror, their hands lifting to cover their faces.

I urged Taen toward Brunt, not stopping my shayde until he'd knocked the other male to the wooden floor.

"Dakur," Nia cried, stretching her hand out to me, her face cratered with a determination that told me she'd wrench me away from Taen and hide me behind her. Then she'd face the beast with only her bare hands to protect me.

As always, my mate amazed me. Even when faced with a terrifying creature, she only thought of me.

Still caging Brunt with his enormous, clawed feet, Taen turned his head toward Nia.

He licked her hand, and she gave both Taen and me a tremulous smile.

I held my hand out to Nia. "I believe it's time for us to leave, my pretty mate."

I tossed the bags toward the center of the arena.

CHAPTER 23
NIA

As I grabbed Dakur's hand, and he pulled me up to sit in front of him on the beast, a loud bang erupted in the arena, followed by shaking.

A big hole appeared in the middle of the fighting area, and sand started sliding down into it. The stands shook, and I looked up, worried the entire structure was about to collapse.

"Go," I cried.

I marveled at how Dakur could make the beast respond to his commands, how it seemed to know him.

"Nia, my love?" Dakur purred. "I'd like to introduce you to my friend, Taen."

"The beast is a Taen?"

"This shayde is my friend, and his name is Taen." He leaned forward and rasped in my ear. "I saved him. Raised him. He's about to save *us*."

"We need to get out of here," I shouted as the stands started to sway. People shrieked and raced for the exits.

Dakur guided the creature to leap back over the high fence and bound toward the gate on the right. The guards standing beside it took one look at Taen and shrieked, scattering in all directions.

Dakur brought Taen to a skidding halt in front of the gate and roared at the quivering guard standing against the wall on the right. "Let us out, or I'll send the shayde after you."

"Yes," the man cried. "On it immediately Sir. Boss." He shook his head. "Orc. Whatever!" He raced to the latch and unlocked it, dragging the enormous metal structure to the right, clearing the path to the tunnel beyond.

A glance over my shoulder showed Brunt shoving his way through the crowd as he made his way down the stairs to the stand's exit. His face florid with rage, his gaze remained locked on us.

"We've got to get out of here," I said. "My step-brother will find a way to stop us."

The shayde raced through the long tunnel.

Dakur brought him to a halt when we reached the intersection leading to the cages, and I slipped off.

"I'm releasing everyone else," I cried out. We didn't have time, but how could I leave without giving everyone the same chance as me?

Dakur left Taen and followed me as I ran down the hallway between the cages but came to a shuddering halt when I found Veegar ahead, watching us.

With a grin, he held up a ring of keys. "Ready to free

some beasts? I released everyone but those I didn't dare go near."

Rushing toward him, I snatched them from his grip.

In no time, I'd unlocked the chains keeping my beast friends pinned to walls. They bounded past us with Veegar pressing his back against the wall, his eyes wild and Dakur ducking inside a cage opening to watch. He ran to his own cage and emerged with blades in sheaths strapped around his thighs.

When everyone was free, we ran back to Taen and mounted once more.

"Go," Veegar called out. "I'll tell them you went west."

He must know we'd head north, toward the forest.

I wanted to hug him but there wasn't time.

"Thank you, friend," Dakur said. "You have a place at my fire and with the Matis Clan whenever you have need. Remember." He touched two fingers to his forehead and dipped his head down.

"I'll remember." Veegar hurried back into the hallway.

"How do we get out of here?" Dakur called out by my ear.

"Keep going straight. At the intersection, take the stone channel on the right. It slopes up to the ground level and while there's a gate there to keep anyone from entering the arena without paying, it's our only way out."

His arm snug around my waist, Dakur leaned forward, urging Taen for more speed.

My pulse thundered in time with the pad of his big paws, and my lungs raged. If we could get past that final gate, we might stand a chance of escaping.

"Once we're out, we need to head to the eastern side of the village," I said over my shoulder.

Around us, beasts snarled and gnashed their fangs, but they left us alone. Like creatures escaping a fiery blaze, we all had one focus, getting out of here alive.

Shouts echoed down the long tunnel, and the stomp of many feet chased us. The guards would do all they could to do as Brunt demanded, or they'd feel his wrath. But I was done obeying him, of acting as if my needs didn't matter.

It was time for me to escape him and finally live.

We reached the intersection and Taen skidded around the corner, going right while the other creatures followed. They knew I'd helped them; they trusted me to do so once more.

With long leaps, Taen clawed his way up the channel rising toward the surface. Light bloomed ahead, and for a moment, I began to believe we'd make it, that we'd find the gate open and no one there to stop us.

The gate *was* open, and we burst through into the cool night with beasts leaping around us. Stars peppered the inky blackness overhead, but the moon hadn't risen to help guide our way. No matter. I knew where we needed to go, at least for the first part of our journey.

Creatures we'd freed raced away to the left, perhaps smelling the water they'd find at the oasis. They'd flee into the desert after that, and I wished them well.

We were all on our own now.

"Which direction?" Dakur called out, his head jerking to the left and right wildly. An alley stretched ahead of us with buildings on both sides, the smithy warehouse on the left, and Brunt's other businesses on the right. No one worked at this time of night.

"That way." I pointed to the end of the alley. "Once we're past the buildings, turn left and keep going all the way to the end of the village. We'll have to circle around to the right and enter the desert to collect my things, but after that, we're free and can head north."

His arm tightened around me, and he nudged Taen's sides. The beast burst forward, and I was grateful to see he didn't limp. Perhaps my care had helped him heal enough he'd be able to take us on this long journey. It would pass much quicker if we could ride.

We skidded to a halt at the end of the alley.

Brunt stood there with what looked like all his men. They were well-armed and prepared to battle an army.

Brunt lifted a crossbow and pointed it at us.

CHAPTER 24
DAKUR

"Release Nia, and I'll let you go, Dakur," Brunt snarled.

Another deal he could renege on? "When it comes to my mate's safety, I don't bargain."

"Mate?" He sneered. "She'll never be yours. Nia," he barked. "Get off the shayde and come to me." Juggling the crossbow to his right arm, he stretched out his left hand as if he expected her to slide off Taen and placidly walk over to join him.

She lifted her chin. "Let me go. I'm not going to let you sell me."

"You belong to me!"

"I. Belong. To. Myself!"

"I'm going to send Taen through them," I whispered by her ear. "Hold on."

A nudge of my heels, and Taen burst into speed. Only Brunt held his stance. The others scattered, yelping in terror. Brunt leveled the crossbow, and his finger twitched on the trigger. One tap of my heel on Taen's right side, and he jerked out of the way of the bolt, still rushing toward Brunt.

Brunt cried out and flung himself to the side of the alley.

We shot past him with spears and blades clattering on the street around us. A few made glancing blows on Taen, but his thick, scaled hide deflected them all. Miraculously, none hit me or Nia, but I suspected Brunt's order was to slow us down, not kill us.

Not Nia anyway.

At my urging, Taen rushed to the left, bounding down the street while the few people out tonight gasped and either slunk inside buildings or plastered themselves against the walls. They gaped at the beast thundering past them before hurrying in the opposite direction.

At the end of the road, I spied the beginnings of the desert sand with straggling spurts of grass. No trees or other vegetation in sight. This wouldn't be an easy crossing. While Taen could run for a long time, that had always been in the cool forest, never in the heat of the sun or without water. I couldn't imagine how he made his way across such a great expanse on his own.

Nia pointed. "We need to get to that pile of rocks. I've got a hidden cache there."

My groan of self-loathing rang out. "I should've found a way to collect provisions."

"How?" She glanced up at me before looking forward again. "Were you going to save half the bread Brunt reluctantly fed you? Some of the brackish water?"

"You knew."

"I snuck you whatever food I could. I suspect Veegar did too."

"I appreciated everything you brought me. Him as well." I hugged her against my chest, grateful we'd escaped the compound and had hope of finally putting it and Brunt behind us. "Without those meals, I would've starved."

"Brunt's stupid. If he fed his fighters, they'd do better, but he's much too greedy to share anything with those who make him money."

We reached the pile of rocks, and I brought Taen to a stop. While I scanned the area for threats, not seeing anything of concern, she slid off the shayde's back and hurried around to the other side of the pile.

I dismounted and followed, my legs stiff already. It had been a long time since I'd ridden a shayde, but I'd tighten back up over the next week or so.

What worried me most was Nia. She wore a skirt, and her legs were bare beneath. They'd rub against Taen's scales, and she'd be raw in no time.

I helped Nia shift aside a pile of rocks and dig into the sand, exposing a large metal box I lifted out of the hole for her.

She unlocked it and opened the top to reveal packages and an empty sack beneath that she started loading with what she'd hidden. "This is six months' worth of hiding food and supplies."

"I have these." I gestured to the blades I'd strapped to my thighs. "Veegar brought them for me earlier."

"I suspect he knew I'd run soon." The sack now full, she rocked back on her heels, looking up at me. "I wish there was more, but there's enough food here for a few days."

"We'll find a way to survive." I tugged her up and held her. "As long as we have each other, nothing else matters."

"Your belly might say otherwise when the food runs out," she said with a low laugh.

"I've never hunted in the desert, but there must be prey of one sort or another. Taen will hunt and bring back what he doesn't finish himself." He'd done this in the forest, showing up with half a carcass, presenting it to me with pride.

"We'll find snakes, probably. Bugs." She shrugged and turned in my embrace, looking up at me. "We should head toward one of the oasises. We can restock our supplies and rest there."

"How long will it take to reach the first?"

"Three days heading north." She frowned. "I've heard orcs use them as well. I don't know how many humans do. But if the oasis is occupied, we can hide until they leave."

"Do you think Brunt's arm reaches that far?"

"We have to assume so, though he won't know which direction we'll take. He might think we're hiding in the village. Few would challenge the desert even if they had a beast like Taen with them." Her gaze swept the area, though even with moonlight, it was hard to see far, and a shiver tracked through her body. "There are creatures out there you can't imagine, even in your worst nightmare."

"We'll stand guard at all times when we rest."

"If we travel at night, it'll be cold, but we'll avoid some of the creatures who hunt only during the day. And if we can't see far, neither can Brunt. It'll be too hot to travel during the day anyway. I'll help keep watch as much as I can, though I've only heard of the beasts who hunt the desert. I've never seen them." She looked toward the village lights winking in the distance. "Brunt's powerful and many respect him. Maybe not him, per se, but his money and his power. If someone sees us, they'll tell him. If I know Brunt, he'll put out the word that I'm on the run. He'll offer a reward for my capture and . . ."

She didn't need to say it. I already knew.

Tilting her chin up, I met her gaze, smoky warm in the moonlight. "Try not to worry about what he'll do if he finds us."

"It's hard not to. He'll capture me, but he'll *kill* you, Dakur."

"We're going to escape. I promise you this." He kissed me quickly, cupping my face after and staring into my eyes. When we gazed at each other like this, I felt invincible. There was nothing we couldn't do together. No one could stop us. Not even Brunt.

I didn't want Dakur worrying about my emotions. I'd deal with them just as I always did, by setting them aside to be brought out to dwell on when I wasn't in danger. For now, our first goal was to put as much distance between us and the village.

He took my hand and led me over to Taen, who'd followed him around the pile of rocks.

"He didn't run away," I said as Dakur secured my bag to a spike jutting up from Taen's spine where his neck met his shoulders. I'd held onto it to maintain my balance while we hurried across the first small stretch of the desert.

"He won't." Dakur went around to Taen's head and

held his cheeks, kissing the beast's forehead. "He missed me. I raised him and his two siblings from the time they were little. Their mother was killed, and I found them mewling under some bushes."

"He's such a glorious, ferocious creature. He was injured when he was captured, and I treated his wound." I waved to the scabbed area on his leg, though it wasn't easy to see in the dark. "That's why he licked me in the arena. He remembered me."

"Him and his siblings aren't like other shaydes. They're brutally vicious. Never doubt that. But they were raised in my clan like true members, and they love us as much as we do them."

"How do you think he ended up here?" I carefully stroked Taen's head, and he purred, nuzzling my belly. He could kill me with the swipe of his paw or one bite, yet he was gentle, like a chall one might adopt and take to bed each night.

"I assume he caught my scent and followed. I'm grateful he did, because with him, we stand a much better chance of making it across the desert."

Taking my hand, Dakur led me to Taen's side.

"I'm more used to riding than you." I had her feel the thicker skin on my inner thighs I'd built up through the years riding our shaydes. "You're much more tender in this area."

I'd already noticed a mild irritation there, and we'd only traveled a short distance. "I'll build thick skin too."

"Not quickly. The process can be painful. I had blisters for weeks when I first started riding them. I had to stop and let myself heal before trying again. Over and over until my body was ready to ride for long distances. We don't have that time for you."

"Cut my skirt." I held it wide. "If you slice down the middle, we can tie the fabric around each leg. That should help somewhat." If I had leather, I could wrap it around my legs, but that wasn't something I thought of hiding in my cache.

"That's a good idea. We'll also change your position frequently. I'll hold you at first, and you'll ride on my thighs."

As he sliced down the middle of my skirt and bound the sides to my legs with thin pieces cut from the hem, my body stirred with the memory of when we were together. He straightened, and I teased a finger down his chest. "I'm always happy to ride your thighs." My voice choked off with desire I shouldn't be feeling at a time like this. But we were alive. We'd escaped Brunt's grip so far. And we had hope for a future together.

"You, mate, are a welcome tease." He kissed me again, pressing my back against Taen's side, and I couldn't hold back my moan. He lifted his head too quickly. "One day soon, we'll be together again. I need you." The hoarseness of his voice sunk through me, licking across my core. He tapped my nose. "For now, we ride, and we ride fast."

I nodded, and he lifted me up onto Taen's back, both of my legs on one side, following me with an easy leap. He lifted me onto his thighs and wrapped his arm around me.

"North," he said.

"North." I pointed to a bright star on the horizon. "Aim in that direction."

With a nudge of his heels, he guided Taen out into the desert with only the moonlight and one star to guide our way.

I didn't look back at the village.

CHAPTER 26
DAKUR

We couldn't push Taen long or we'd stress his body. He wasn't used to running in the desert, even if it was cooler at night.

After a few hours, we stopped near a cluster of dusky plants that wouldn't generate enough shade to make it worth walking over to stand beneath them during daylight hours. At night, they wouldn't hold back an attacking chall, and the tiny, fluffy creatures some kept as pets could be nudged away with a finger.

"Here's something I learned that might help us." Nia strode across the sand, her steps slow due to the slippery surface. She stood beside one of the larger plants, gesturing for me to join her.

Moonlight cut down through the sky, and while she was partly in shadow, my eyes had adjusted to the lack of light.

I watched as she sliced through one of the plant's

limbs with a kitchen blade she'd stolen. She took care not to let the sharp spikes jutting from the tan plant surface cut her hand as she held it. Once severed, she whacked off each spike with the hilt of the blade and held a thick piece of plant toward me.

"It's wet inside," she said. "Especially when the juices flow up to the top of the plant at night. It's not a lot of fluid, but it will be enough for us." She cut it in half and beat on the inner surface made up of thin strands. Juice glistened in the depression she'd made, and she tipped it up over her mouth, letting the drops glide down onto her tongue.

I did the same, licking what was left like she did after sucking all the juice from the spongy insides. It tasted mildly sweet and green. There was no other way to describe it.

"I wonder . . ." she said after we'd drank from and discarded numerous chunks of plant. Stooping down, she used her hands to scoop aside sand at the base of the largest plant. The sand got thicker, and I helped her, digging down to the depth of my forearm.

"It's damp," I said, seeing where she was going with this.

She nodded. "I assumed the plant must suck what bit of moisture it can from beneath the desert's surface. It does rain here, though not often. If we dig far enough, we might find water for Taen. Would he drink it?"

The shayde had wandered over to join us and stood nearby, breathing heavier than I liked.

"It's worth trying."

We widened the hole, making sure to move the sand far enough away from where we'd dug to keep it from sliding back into the hold. We lost precious water ourselves in sweat as we kept working, but this cluster of plants should have enough liquid in its limbs to replace what we lost.

When she couldn't reach any longer, I gently dropped her down into the hole. She continued to move the now damp sand up and toss it a distance from the opening while I did the same, though I could still do so while kneeling on the ground.

Finally, we were rewarded with a small pool of water winking at us in the moonlight.

"Yes," Nia breathed, looking up at me with so much happiness, it made my breath catch.

I grinned right back, marveling at how such a simple thing as water could make both of us happy.

"I'm not sure Taen can reach," Nia said. "There's a small bowl in the pack. Give it to me, and I'll scoop up water for him to drink."

In a short time, Taen was eagerly slurping the water from the bowl. It wasn't a lot, but it was better than nothing.

We drank more from the plant and feeling refreshed, remounted Taen, riding until dawn winked on the horizon. We stopped and repeated the process, drinking from a plant while digging deeply to expose the water among the roots. I could tell we weren't replenishing the moisture we lost from our journey, but it was better than nothing. There had been no way to bring jugs with us.

"We should stop soon," she said, peering around. Finally, she pointed. "There's a mound over there. We might find a place out of the sun to wait until it's night again."

I trusted her knowledge of this area of our world. I was used to moving through the cool forest, to hunting creatures only found there and drinking from streams and rivers. The desert was as foreign to me as the arena had been. I had the strength of an orc, but she understood ways to survive in this part of our world.

We led Taen across the shifting sands toward the mound, and it surprised me how long it took to reach it. Distance was hard to gauge here. It was difficult to see among the shadows.

Sunrise had dragged up heat along with it, and we were soon gasping.

Eventually, we reached the small hill and climbed it, pausing on the top where the wind had blown the stone surface clean.

"This will be a good place to stop," she said, biting down on her lower lip and scanning the area. "I know we're easy to see when we're this high, but during the day, large creatures erupt from the sand. They're like snakes only much bigger. They'll eat us." She stomped on the smooth stone underfoot. "But they don't burrow in this."

"Let me look around the outside of the mound to see if we can hide a bit better."

She nodded. "I don't know much about the desert. I was born in the village, and I've never traveled beyond my rock cluster where I hid my supplies. All I know comes from stories. Veegar was a soldier, and he spoke a lot about the desert. I wish I'd paid more attention to what he said, because there was a lot to learn from his harrowing tales."

"You couldn't know how vital his stories would be."

"Now I do." Her lips lifted briefly before smoothing. "I'll miss him. He was one of my few friends. When my parents died, I only had Lana and Veegar." Her fingers traced across her face, and I wasn't sure she realized she did it. I'd caught her touching her scars on more than one occasion when she was lost in the past.

She explained how Lana helped her, and I hoped one day to pay her friend back for her kindness. She'd taken a risk for my mate, and I'd be grateful forever.

"I'm glad you had them," I said.

"He helped you too. Maybe he could tell I cared for you, though I didn't let on to anyone that I love you."

"Mate," I said, tugging her into my arms and holding her. We were safe for now, and I savored how wonderful it was to be with her without the shadow of fear hanging over us.

Too soon, I left her to climb down the rocky side of the hill and look around. She sat at the top with Taen to wait. He'd wanted to follow me but remained when I told him how much I love her and how vital it was that he remain behind to protect her.

I hoped to find a cave or even a shallow depression

where we could rest out of the sun, but I didn't. Returning to the top, I dropped down beside her, putting my arm around her shoulders.

"The sun won't shine in the same area all day," I said. "Judging by where it's rising, this area," I pointed to my right, "will be in shadows within a short time."

Nothing moved for as far as I could see, which was a comfort. Perhaps we could sleep for a bit before we took turns at watch.

We got up, and I led her to the area I'd found where we could put stone behind and beneath us. Was this enough protection from the large snakes she'd described? I hoped so. I only had my blades and Taen to defend us.

"It's as good a place to rest as any," she said, settling on the ground.

Taen sighed and laid across the front of us, staring out into the vast desert.

I joined Nia, this time pulling her onto my lap and holding her. Soon, it would be too hot to snuggle, but in the chilly dawn, it was amazing to be close to her.

"One more night's travel," she said. "And we'll reach the first oasis. I've heard there are many scattered throughout the desert, and again, I wish I'd paid more attention when the older men spoke of their travels."

"We're going to do this." I had complete confidence we'd not only survive but also reach my clan. "You've already made a huge difference with the plants." I patted Taen's shoulder. "Taen's not missing out either."

"Even in the village, we had to be careful with water.

A bath was rare, and only the wealthiest could afford them. The rest of us washed in basins or snuck down to the pool you mentioned in the lower level of the compound."

"Did Brunt build the pool?"

"It was there when he bought the building, though crumbled. Water seeps down from the large oasis pool and some makes it way there. He had his men reconstruct the bathing tub and uses it himself quite often. He only rarely allowed me down there."

"He's a horrible person."

"Greedy and self-centered. The oasis our village is built near is large, one of the biggest in the desert, I've heard, but it's not endless. I've tried to imagine lakes or the ocean, but I can't picture bodies of water that big."

"Rivers of cool water flow through the forest, and we'll travel to the orc kingdom and splash in the sea. I have friends who live on islands far from shore, plus others who live close to the water. We can stay with them and enjoy seeing everything the city has to offer."

"Will your clan and those living in the orc city welcome me or . . ."

"You'll be as treasured by them as by me. Females are rare among orcs. Many were killed years ago during a shayde attack, and fewer are born all the time. Some orcs have taken human mates. When we travel to the city, you'll meet them. They're happy, thriving, and bearing young. Their orc husbands adore them."

"It would be lovely to be welcome somewhere."

She sounded so wistful, and I wanted to tell her she'd

be cherished, not only by me. Each female brought to the clan was a treasured piece of our future, whether she could bear young or not.

Nia would soon see.

She yawned.

"Sleep," I said. "I'll hold you and keep watch. Taen will alert us if anyone comes near."

"You need to sleep too."

"I'll rest once you have. We have all day."

"Alright. Wake me by midday so I can keep watch while you sleep."

"I will." Perhaps. She wasn't used to traveling on a shayde while I was. I could doze while we rode tonight, and she would wake me if there was any concern.

She fell asleep quickly, and despite the growing heat, I held my precious mate, watching her face. She must've dreamed, because she smiled, and I hoped she thought of our future.

Waking in the afternoon, she stretched. By then, I'd laid her on the blanket I took from the pouch.

She sat up and peered around, shoving her hair off her face. "You didn't wake me."

"You were tired."

Peering up at me, she frowned. "And you look exhausted. We have a few hours before we'll leave. Sleep." She tugged the bag close and pulled out one of the pouches of food she'd sealed in greased paper to keep bugs from getting into it. Unfolding it, she held out a seed and berry cake and took one for herself, placing the rest back in the pouch and folding the wrapper around it again.

We ate quickly, and I laid down on the blanket, drifting to sleep. I woke as the sun was scooping a hold in the horizon to bury itself and looked around, thankful to see Taen lying nearby and nothing moving in the desert. Nia's smiling face was the most welcome sight in the world.

After eating again, we hung our pack on Taen's shoulder spike and mounted, Nia facing me this time, sitting on my thighs with her legs wrapped around me to change the pressure points.

I urged Taen out into the desert, though we stopped at the first cluster of liquid-giving plants we found, making sure Taen also got plenty to drink.

We traveled all night, stopping periodically to drink from the plants, and when dawn heralded a new day, I spied the oasis ahead, a shimmer of green and blue on the horizon.

Stopping near a low hill some distance from it, we dismounted and sat on the top of the hill to study the area.

"We need to watch for a while to make sure no one else is there," Nia whispered. "If someone's using the oasis, we'll have to wait until they leave."

I nodded, but I saw no movement ahead.

I wasn't sure what alerted me. Maybe it was the subtle sound of shifting sand behind us. Or the way Taen froze and stopped breathing. Or the trickle of sand crystals landing on my shoulder.

Unsheathing a blade, I rose and spun, staring up at the enormous snake looming over us.

Fangs bared; it snapped its head toward us.

Nia screamed. I grabbed her and tumbled to the right as the snake's head struck the rocky sand.

CHAPTER 27

NIA

Dakur rolled and came up to his feet with me in his arms. He pushed me behind him and stepped forward with only a blade to defend us.

I grabbed a handful of sand to throw, though I knew it wouldn't make much difference, if any at all. The creature was probably used to getting sand in its eyes.

Two stories tall, it undulated in front of us, its copper scaled hide gleaming in the early morning light. Its head whipped back and forth, and it stared at us as if it could lull us with its weaving dance.

Taen burst into speed, leaping toward the snake. He sprung up and latched onto the creature's neck with his long teeth, but the snake shook and Taen went flying. He landed hard in the sand on his side and struggled to get to his feet.

"No!" I rushed toward the snake, flinging the sand.

Dakur grabbed me around the waist as I passed and pushed me toward the dubious safety of the hill. "Get around the other side and hide." Without waiting to see if I'd do as he asked, he ran toward the snake.

"Stay out of the way," Dakur barked at Taen. "Watch Nia."

Taen hobbled over to me, standing between me and the snake, growling.

The beast snapped out again, and Dakur dove to the side, rolling and rising quickly to his feet. He flung the blade, and it pierced the snake between the eyes. The creature shrieked and flipped its head back and forth, dislodging the blade. With a snarl, it advanced on Dakur, who backed toward me.

"Run, Nia," he hissed. "Hide!"

I spun and raced along the base of the hill but stopped some distance away.

Dakur faced the snake bravely.

He did something I'd only seen him do once, while in the arena just before we escaped. Then, I couldn't figure out what happened. Now, I watched as he lifted his pendant and blew across it.

A low hum shimmered through the air.

The snake paused and stared at it as if it was now the one being lulled. Releasing a shriek, it dove backward and burrowed into the sand.

I ran to Dakur and wrapped my arms around him.

He rubbed my back. "You're not hurt?"

"It didn't come near me. What about you?"

"I'm fine."

We backed until we reached the side of the hill.

"What did you do?" I asked. "I swear you did something that made it flee."

He clasped his pendant. "Our clan fates are our saviors. My people learned how to generate sounds with a breath across our pendants. We use the tones for practical things like asking plants to shoot us up into the canopy."

He was going to have to show me that one day soon.

"We also use them to control creatures, sometimes prey we're hunting for meat. When I was young, I studied with the wanderers, orcs who travel to learn new tones to teach the clan. Back in the arena, I used my pendant to release my chains, a tone I'd discovered and practiced while in my cage. I didn't know a sound that would make the desert snake leave, and honestly, I just blew across it, hoping to luck into a tone that might make it pause."

"It's magic."

He shrugged. "Who can understand the fates? But I think the sound irritated it, and that's why it left."

"Whatever you did, you saved us both." I stretched out my hand to Taen who'd crept near, limping on his front right leg but otherwise appearing unharmed.

I stooped down and examined his paw, but I didn't find any injury, just a place where he huffed when I touched it. No swelling yet.

"Maybe he hit it on a rock when he fell," I said.

"That must be it." Dakur grabbed our pack that had fallen off Taen when he jumped toward the snake. "We should go to the oasis as quickly as we can."

"It'll be safer even if someone else is there."

We cautiously climbed the hill and studied the green and blue area ahead again but didn't see any movement before crossing the sand with Taen limping beside us.

"We'll need to remain at the oasis while he rests," I said. Hopefully, his injury would be healed by the time we needed to leave. If not, we could find a place to hide in case anyone else stopped for respite before continuing when Taen could once again carry us.

Dakur put his arm around me and tucked me against his side, leaning over to kiss the top of my head. "I'm looking forward to the short break with you, mate."

I smiled up at him. "We can swim, something I've only done a few times."

"I can't wait."

The sand gave way to scruffy, tan grass, and then the big slabs of smooth rock that surrounded the oasis. Trees had found a way to grow through the cracks in the rock, and even tiny flowers had found purchase in bits of rotted vegetation. We wove among the trees until we reached a thicker forest, though nothing like what Dakur had described when he talked about his home. Holding hands, we found a path etching toward the big pool that gleamed in the sunshine.

"Even though I grew up in a village built near an oasis similar to this," I said, "I still marvel that a body of water isn't swallowed up by the surrounding sand."

"It's a gift from the fates."

"Something to be treasured."

We reached the shore of the pool and Taen drank a

long while before flopping in the cool grass growing along the bank that stretched to scruffy woods twenty feet or so away. Taen sighed, and I was grateful again we'd escaped the snake and that no one had been badly hurt.

Dakur and I also drank, and my belly soon sloshed when I moved.

I wasn't looking forward to traveling through the desert again. That wouldn't be the last snake to attack. If one came near, I hoped Dakur would be able to recreate the sound with his pendant.

Dakur hung our bag of food on a low tree limb and returned to stand beside me, staring at the oasis.

The pool was oblong and a clear teal blue. So beautiful I couldn't describe it. Vegetation grew along most of the sides. I pointed. "I bet I'll find tubers we can eat."

A fish splashed, and Dakur grinned. "Now I almost feel at home. I'll catch a fish to add to your tubers."

My belly rumbled in anticipation already.

We split up, though we remained in sight of each other, and I dug clusters of tubers while he waded into the water and stood very still. His hand darted down into the water and lifted it, clutching a squirming fish. He tossed it onto the shore, and Taen grunted and rose, limping over to snatch it up and gobble it down with one bite.

"I'd better catch a lot of fish," Dakur said with a laugh.

Returning to where Taen had laid back down to wait for more fish, I washed the tubers and placed them nearby to serve with our fish. They tasted wonderful cooked and with butter, but they could also be eaten raw.

Dakur caught three more fish for Taen and four for us.

"I'll clean them and start a fire after our swim," he said, joining me on the shore.

"I'm hot. I'm going to jump into the water," I declared, tugging at the hem of my blouse. "I'll wash my clothing and drape everything on branches to dry." At least I had another outfit to wear or . . .

I slid a look Dakur's way.

His hands froze on the fish, and he looked up, his gaze darkening as it met mine.

"I believe I know what you're thinking, mate," he said with a curl of his lips.

"We live. We love. I'm eager to celebrate that fact, *mate*." I tugged my blouse off and tossed it aside to be washed. My skirt soon followed. Without looking at Dakur again, though I caught his breath hissing out in excitement, I splashed into the water until it covered my breasts.

I turned to face him, treading my legs. "I think you should finish cleaning those fish." I gave him a sultry smile. "My mate needs to make love to me as soon as possible."

CHAPTER 28

DAKUR

I'd never cleaned fish this fast before. Leaving the portion we'd eat inside a piece of greased paper I found in our sack, I quickly tossed aside my loincloth and, with a stiff cock already, strode into the water to join Nia.

She met me partway, her fingertips teasing across my shoulders.

"Dakur." Her legs wound around my body as we floated, and she rubbed herself against my stiff cock.

I lifted her and slanted my mouth across hers. I'd never get enough of my mate. She was my light. My strength. The only person who could make me feel whole.

She gasped against my mouth, her lips parting, and I stroked her tongue with mine.

While she rocked against me, the juncture between her thighs teasing the head of my erect cock, I held her. Treasured her. I wove my fingers into the damp tendrils of her hair and stroked the back of her neck, burying my fingers within her thick strands to angle her head for my kiss.

I lifted my head, staring down at her with so much love, I wasn't sure my heart could handle any more.

"You're perfect," I said, stroking my fingertips across her face.

She didn't cringe when I touched her scars, and I was grateful she seemed to finally see the woman I adored. Nia was beautiful both inside and out, and I was grateful she felt comfortable in my love.

While Taen sighed and moved to higher ground, facing away from us where he'd naturally keep watch, I moved my fingers down Nia's neck to her breast.

She clung to my shoulders, still moving against me, her eyes locked on mine.

"You're everything, Dakur," she whispered. "I mean it. I'll love you until the day I die and beyond. No one will ever take your place in my heart, and when we're nothing but mist in the air, I'll still seek you. I'll coil around you and hold tight, and when the sun rises to burn off our mist, we'll float into the sky together."

"Nia," I groaned, my heart aching from her words. While I rolled her hardened nipple, I kissed her again, showing her I felt the same.

My heart roared in my ears, and while supporting her body with a hand on her butt, I slid my other hand between her legs.

She bucked against me, moaning, and there wasn't a

purer sound than that. May I hear it every day for the rest of my life.

I only came alive when I was with her, and it would be that way forever.

Lifting my head, I watched the expressions on her face while sliding a finger inside her tight passage.

"Yes," she hissed. "Like that."

I stroked her clit with my thumb while pumping two fingers inside her, stretching her to receive my cock once more.

When I sensed she was near, I carried her to the shore and laid her in the soft grass.

"I need you, Dakur." She held out her arms.

"Like this, pretty mate." I rolled her onto her belly and lifted her hips, centering my cock at her opening.

She mewed and rocked back against me.

Holding her hips steady, I pressed forward, burying my cock deep inside her.

NIA

I felt like we were doing this for the very first time. The position was new, but that wasn't why. Our love had only grown stronger, culminating in this moment when we could finally be together without fear. We'd escaped the compound, and in this, we were both free to relax and explore each other.

The sensation of his body moving within mine lit me on fire. I loved this orc with everything inside me and showing him became my only focus. That he could find pleasure in my body only made this better.

"You're amazing," he growled. "So perfect. My mate. My love. My entire world." While one hand held me in place, he pulled his cock out and drove it back inside. The stretch was almost too much, but I craved the burn. Craved him.

His fingers stroked my back, and his second cock somehow stretched around to latch onto my clit. Could anything be better than this male loving me so completely? I didn't think so, but I knew if anyone could show me, it would be Dakur.

I rocked back against him, urging him to go faster. My mind kept swirling, getting lost in the sensations, and I wasn't sure I could hold off much longer. That sucking motion on my clit . . . It drove me wild.

His fingers digging into my hips, holding me in place for each drive forward, made my heart shatter. He went faster, so fast I couldn't keep up. I could only hold on and feel.

Heat blazed higher and higher inside me as he growled and told me how beautiful I was, how amazing I made him feel, how he adored the feel of my body sucking so tightly on his cock.

"Dakur," I cried, pleading with him for something I couldn't define. What we shared eclipsed everything around us. All I could focus on was his thick cock thrusting inside me and his second cock swirling across my clit like a tongue.

I was so close . . .

"You're mine, Nia. Mine," he groaned, his hips moving impossibly fast, pushing me even higher.

"Mine," I growled right back. "Mine, Dakur. Always."

And with that, I fell apart, pieces of me blasting outward before sliding back in to put me back together again.

Shuddering above me, he shouted out his satisfaction.

He kept moving, though slower and deeper, drawing

out our pleasure until I was rocked through another climax.

When I couldn't take any more, he wrapped his arms around me and dropped to the side, taking me with him. He lifted his upper body and kissed the side of my neck.

"You're my precious one," he said. "There will never be another for me. I'll love you from the moment you wake until the world cycles through once more, and then until we take our final breaths."

"Dakur," I said, leaning back into his embrace. "I love you. You're my only reason for existing, the light in my darkness and the warmth in my soul."

"Mate," he whispered into my hair. "My perfect mate."

His big cock twitched inside me, stiffening once more. He pulled out and gently rolled me onto my back, lifting my legs up onto his shoulders. "Let me taste us, taste you."

When he buried his face between my thighs, I thrust up to meet him.

We washed in the pool and dressed, then ate, feeding each other, teasing with strokes of our fingers and tongue until we couldn't hold anything back. After, we washed our clothing, me pouting about having to wash so much more than him. We splashed each other and soon, our clothing was tossed aside once more, and we dropped to the ground, entwining our bodies as tightly as our hearts.

Dressed once more, we slept and woke at dusk. Seeing that Taen was no longer limping, we filled our water flasks, packed our things, and set out again, walking beside the shayde for a bit before testing his leg with us riding. When his gait remained steady, we kept going, stopping only to cut plants for liquid and dig beneath them for Taen to drink.

Other than stopping to rest, eat, and drink, we kept going, knowing we had two more night's travel before we'd reach the next oasis. At dawn, we found a somewhat shady place to rest, and I urged him to sleep while I stood guard because I'd dozed in his arms while we rode.

Somehow, I nodded off again.

I woke to Brunt and his men surrounding us. Taen wasn't in sight, and I couldn't imagine where he could be.

Even Veegar was there with a big, handprint bruise on his face and brown eyes full of sadness.

Brunt leveled his crossbow on Dakur and fed me a slick grin.

"Time to go home, stepsister. If we leave now, we'll make it back in time for the auction."

CHAPTER 30
DAKUR

Growling, I sprung to my feet, sand falling away from my clothing, and urged Nia behind me. We'd stopped along the base of another rocky hill and settled in what felt like a secure spot with stone behind and beneath us.

It was clear no place was safe from Brunt.

But I wasn't going to let him take Nia back to that nightmare again. Even if it took me sacrificing my life, I'd keep it from happening.

I leaped at Brunt like a shayde on prey, my legs launching me through the oppressive desert heat. Brunt had barely enough time to grunt in surprise before I slammed into him. Hitting him squarely, I dragged him down hard in the sand.

He snarled, snapping his head out to impact with mine, and I saw stars as we rolled, grappling, sand kicking up around us. Only one of us was going to come out of this battle, whoever had the most muscle and will, and I was determined that person would be me.

I'd heard he not only enjoyed watching fights, but he also regularly battled himself. His reflexes proved sharper than I'd given him credit for. As we came to a stop with him beneath me, his fist came rocketing up toward my face. The punch connected solidly with my jaw; the force reverberated through my skull and driving my tusks against the tender flesh inside my mouth.

For a moment, there was nothing but blinding pain and the coppery tang of blood coating my throat. But I was an orc, trained to fight to the death, and I had the determination of the multiple caedos who'd come before me. Only now did I thank my father for insisting I train with his warriors from the time I could walk.

Brunt bucked, kicking out, sending me flying off him to land hard on my back.

His men cheered while Nia cried out my name.

Seeing the tears on her face and the way she huddled against the side of the hill brought me to my senses.

Pain stoked the rage within me, making me roar as I leaped to my feet, my focus sharp, drilling into him. The desert wind whipped sand into the air, but I barely noticed. My whole world had narrowed down to the man who stood between me and the life I wanted, the woman I needed with every fiber of my being. He'd stolen enough; I wasn't going to let him steal anything more.

Nia and I would walk away from this battle free, and this male would no longer follow.

Brunt braced himself for my charge. As I smacked

into him, his fist came up, catching me in the jaw again, reminding me he was no soft village dweller but someone who'd also survived by his strength and wits. I grunted, my tusks scraping against my lip, the taste of blood mixing with the dust in my throat.

I jerked my fist out, impaling him in the face. Bright red blood poured from his nose. I swung out with my leg, sweeping him off his feet, and he tumbled to the side, landing hard. With a groan, he shifted around and jumped to his feet, but he wavered, rubbing the side of his head.

I tackled him, and we grappled, our hands searching for holds on gritty, sweat-slicked skin. The setting sun was a hammer in my head, but its heat was nothing when compared to the fire burning through my veins. Brunt was strong, his blows like steel, but I had something worth fighting for beyond simple victory, my hatred for what he'd done to so many creatures and people. My love for Nia. And my determination to protect her above everything else.

His knee drove into my side, and agony radiated through me. I let out a roar and wrapped my hands around his throat, my pulse slamming in my ears as I tightened my grip. Redness filled his face, and he bucked, trying to dislodge me.

"Give up," I snarled. "Nod to show me you'll leave us alone."

He shook his head and snarled, slamming his fists against my head and shoulders, struggling to knock me away.

Finally, his face started turning blue and his eyes bugged in his head. He slumped beneath me, his hands smacking against the sand.

While the rage roaring through me told me to end this now and forever, I wasn't Brunt. I'd kill in self-defense, but all I wanted was for him to leave us alone.

I rocked up off him and stood over him while he gasped and sputtered, struggling to suck in wind through his bruised throat. My gaze spanned his silent men watching, and I sent them a snarling challenge. Each one looked down or away.

Just as I'd thought.

With a growl of disgust, I turned away, stumbling toward Nia.

Her arms outstretched, she rushed toward me. It was over. If Brunt didn't back away, I'd end it permanently, and he knew it.

As Nia reached me, and a sound behind sent me spinning.

Brunt dove for the crossbow he'd dropped in the sand. He rolled onto his back and sent a bolt flying toward me.

Nia cried out and stepped between us, taking the shot meant for me in her chest.

CHAPTER 31
NIA

Pain. So much pain.

I gaped down at the arrow sticking out of my chest, then looked up at Dakur.

I couldn't breathe. I couldn't think. My heart thudded once. Twice. And I worried it would stop and thud no more.

"Nia," Dakur bellowed, sweeping me up in his arms. "Oh, Nia," he groaned. He looked down at me, and there was so much sadness on his face, it shook me like a beast with a ragdoll in its fangs.

"Dakur," I gasped out. "Dakur. It . . . hurts."

"Hold on, love. Please, hold on." He spun with me in his arms. "Help us. Help her!"

I was the healer, but I couldn't find the strength to help the orc I'd love forever. He was in pain. Why couldn't I fix this?

The world spun, blackness crowding in before reluctantly retreating. Something wet dripped down my sides.

It coated Dakur's hands, and he lifted one, gazing at the bright red blood in complete shock.

"No. No!" He dropped to his knees. "Someone. Please. Help her!"

If only time could stand still.

"I want to . . ." I sucked in a breath but damn, it hurt so much. "I want to see the forest. Feel . . . the cool air. Tell me about it . . . Please?"

"Nia," he groaned, dropped to sit with me cradled in his lap. "My lovely Nia. You're the stars, the moon, the entire world to me. Stay with me. Please."

As our gazes locked, the world melted away until there was only him and me. Our love was like a band stretching between us.

His rough hands cradled me gently. He was so big and powerful. With one swipe, he could destroy almost anything. Yet he'd always been tender with me and Taen.

"It would've been wonderful . . ." I couldn't find the strength to speak, and my mind kept blurring, making the words hard to find. "You have . . . such strength. You'll need to . . . Cling to that. Will you do that . . . for me?"

"Nia, stay with me." He kissed my forehead, claiming my lips and breathing into me as if he could keep me alive just by feeding me the life breath I needed.

"Tell me . . . about . . . the forest," I whispered. "Paint me . . . a picture. Please." I needed to see it. Feel it.

"Oh, Nia." His eyes swam with tears. "Listen love. Cling to my words."

I nodded.

"The trees tower so high," he croaked. Tipping his head back, he roared before his gaze dropped back to me. "Oh, Nia."

"The . . . forest." I wanted to see it before . . .

"You sometimes can't see the tops," he said softly. "The leaves are thick, and the air smells like fresh water and sunshine."

I struggled to give him a smile. "Yes. I . . . see it."

"Imagine standing among giants that reach all the way to the sky, their leafy limbs brushing against one another. So many colors. Not just green but deep blue and sometimes pink, depending on the season. These tall trees rise from a carpet of countless plants, all eager to find the sun's kiss. The air is rich with earthiness and life —a damp perfume filled with whispers of leaves rustling above and creatures shuffling below. Light flickers through the dense canopy in ever-moving patches, painting everything it touches with a golden glow."

I tried to picture it fully, but I couldn't. I'd never been there. Never would be . . .

But I could see the love on Dakur's face, see how much he missed his home, how he ached to share it with me.

In this, he was there already.

"Bird calls echo around you," he whispered. "And the branches creak as the trees sway in the wind. It's music to my heart and soul, and you're going to see it, hear it, Nia."

If only I could.

His eyes, filled with a storm of emotions, remained steady on mine. "Hold on for me, love," he rumbled. "Please."

Veegar stooped down beside us. "We need to get that bolt out. I know some healing, and I'll help."

I suspected it was too late, but I appreciated that my friend wanted to try.

"You'll have to let her go," he said, pointing to the sand.

There were more people here. I could hear them moving, and it sounded like a few of them were fighting. But all I could see was Dakur, the love of my life.

My perfect mate.

He was so sad, and I wanted to make him feel better. Sometimes, things just didn't go the way we wanted. Sometimes, life stole the goodness out of everything. Like it took my mom from me too young. My dad and then my stepfather.

But Dakur was a pure heart, my love, and I wanted him to think of me when he finally returned home to the forest.

"Remember me," I whispered as Veegar spread out the blanket Dakur and I had carried. Dakur gently laid me on the surface.

A loud whoosh rang out, followed by the snarl of a beast.

Taen burst from around the hill and leaped onto Brunt, chittering and roaring as he ripped out my stepbrother's throat.

And the whooshing sound grew louder.

As Dakur kissed my forehead, the world started fading, slipping through my fingers no matter how hard I tried to grab onto it.

I swore I saw enormous birds descending from the sky.

CHAPTER 32
DAKUR

Voxes carrying orcs bristling with weapons flew down from above, landing in a large circle around us.

While Brunt's men dropped their weapons and Taen continued to rip at what was left of Brunt, stone men like the one I'd fought in the arena stomped over to mingle with the voxes.

One of the stone people joined us, sweeping Veegar to the side with a flick of his arm. "Let me see."

Flazant. That was its species. Vague stories from my childhood crowded into my mind, tales my mother would whisper before I went to bed. People born of the boulders around us. Our elders said they were once allies, that we'd go to battle together. This was back when we fought off threats worse than them.

No one knows why we drifted apart. Perhaps those who would kill us had been eliminated. Or the Flazant had moved so far away neither group remembered the other existed.

Veegar backed away, wringing his hands. "Can you help her? I know some healing, but I don't have any supplies. That arrow . . ." His gaze cut to the bloody pile that used to be Brunt.

Taen left the body and came over to drop down beside me. He sighed and nudged her leg, but she didn't respond.

Was she dead already?

She couldn't be. I'd know this.

She lay so still. I wasn't sure I could see her chest rising and falling any longer.

My heart sunk like a stone in water. Everything around me stopped, but inside, loud silence screamed. It felt like someone had punched a hole through my chest where Nia had rested, that sweet wonder of falling in love with the one person who not only understood me but accepted me the way I am.

Breathing was hard; even the air felt heavy with her absence.

I couldn't understand how the world kept moving around me, how the men could still find the will to speak or shift their feet when my entire being was shattering.

"I'm Pirrah," the Flazant said, removing a pack from her spine. "And I brought healing supplies."

I swallowed hard. Was she too late or . . . I had to hold on to hope. Without it, I was as lost as someone who'd wandered in this wretched desert for weeks without finding water or food or a reason to go on.

Numbness wrapped itself around me while memories of Nia flickered in my mind—too sharp and bright against the darkness of her possible loss.

Part of me was gone forever—ripped away without warning. The love that filled every corner of my life echoed hollowly, leaving an unfillable void that hurt with every beat of my heart.

"She's not dead yet," Pirrah said dryly. "Stop mourning her until you have a good reason."

I placed my hand on Nia's shoulder as if maintaining a connection would keep her with me.

"Can you help her?" I rasped, my voice as husky as if I'd been screaming for hours.

"I'm going to try," she said softly. "That's all any of us can do, correct?"

Her dark gaze met mine, and while I found sorrow there, I also saw determination.

She studied the arrow's placement in Nia's chest. With steady hands, she checked around the wound, gently rolling Nia up slightly to look at her back, confirming it was lodged without passing through.

"I need light," she barked, and orcs stepped forward holding whisp lanterns. They blew on them, turning the growing darkness into a circle of daylight.

After cutting Nia's blouse to expose her chest to the early night air, Pirrah grunted and tore a strip of cloth from a larger swath. The pungent scent of herbs filled the air. She pressed around where the arrow was lodged in Nia's chest, staunching the now-sluggish bleeding.

"I need to remove this." She grasped the embedded

shaft gently yet firmly, making sure not to jostle it in a way that might cause any further damage. Looking up, her gaze met mine. "Hold her shoulders."

I moved around to Nia's head and leaned over her. I'd breathe for her if I could. Rip my heart from my chest and place it inside hers to keep her living if I could. Instead, I held onto her shoulders and whispered to her, telling her more about my forest home, describing the flowers, the tiny creatures, and the wonder of the world I wanted to show her.

Pirrah gently pulled the arrow from Nia's chest in one smooth motion. Nia groaned but remained unconscious. Dark blood trickled from the hole in her chest.

After tossing the arrow aside, Pirrah coated the wound with a poultice. "This is lindenmint. I've only known it as a tea but recently learned of its other proper- ties. It'll help prevent infection." She placed a clean, herb-soaked cloth over the wound, then wrapped more clean bandages around Nia's chest to provide compres- sion and hold the poultice in place.

Pirrah rocked back on her heels, her gaze meeting mine. "And now, we wait. If she's stable in the morning, we'll fly."

"Fly?" My wild gaze shot to the voxes shifting in the sand nearby. Brunt's men had fled, leaving only Veegar and Brunt's carcass behind. He shuffled his feet and stared at the sand.

"You and your mate are welcome at the Ember Clan," an orc male said. "I'd be honored to share my fire with you."

"You must be Turren, caedos of the Embers," I said. I vaguely noted his dark hair streaked with Ember green, the way his thick horns curled up across his head. A puckered network of scars covered most of his left arm, and it looked slighter than the right. When he injured it, it must've been very painful.

I'd seen people like me arrive while Taen killed Blunt, but I hadn't looked closely enough to see if I knew them.

Turren dipped his head forward. Seeing my gaze on his arm, he tucked it behind his back, his face darkening. "Many have been seeking you, Dakur, including us."

"You . . . Some of your males were in the audience at the fight." My gaze swept across the Flazants, landing on one male in particular. "And you fought me in the arena. You told me to be ready."

"We were looking for a way to get you out," he said. "I wanted to give you hope. I'm Wambak, by the way, though Brunt knew me as Rock."

"Thank you." I sat and very carefully eased Nia's upper body onto my lap. I had to hold her. If I didn't, I worried she'd stop breathing.

That she wouldn't know I'd be here for her forever.

"My work here is done," Pirrah said, gathering up her things. "The next few hours are critical."

"You're leaving?"

"Resting, Dakur." She sighed. "Merely resting. The minerals inside my stony structure are old. My crystalline innards have solidified more than I like." Wambak helped her stand. "I'll lay down for a while. Please call for me if you have need." She turned, and Wambak gently led her over to where someone else had set up a large hide tent. She went inside, and Wambak turned to stand guard at the front opening.

"I'm sorry," Veegar said. "I wish I could've done more. I tried to stop him but," he gestured to his bruised face, "he discovered I helped you and was angry. He brought me here so I'd see him kill you and capture her. I don't believe I would've survived long enough to make it back to the village."

"You're a good friend. You did all you could." Our escape would've been much harder without his intervention.

"I've got a tent set up," Turren said, waving to another hide structure. "If you think she can be carried, we can lay her inside. It'll be more comfortable. You can both rest."

"Do I dare move her?" I asked no one in particular.

"She's stable," Veegar said. "The arrow's out, and it doesn't appear to have hit anything vital. I'd say you could gently carry her."

I eased out from beneath her and carefully lifted her in my arms, following Turren inside the tent. They'd placed a thick bed of furs on the ground, and I lowered her onto the soft surface.

"We have food," Turren said, his sorrow-filled gaze remaining on Nia. His eyes were an unusual color for an orc, a gold richer than the minerals found deep below the ground.

"I can't eat," I said. "Can't drink."

"You'll do her no good if you pass out."

I growled but took the packet of food he held out, the flask of water, eating a bit and drinking quickly while he watched.

"We'll send word to your mother that we've found you," he said. "She knew you weren't dead."

"My mother has an uncanny way of seeing what's coming next." Had she seen Nia dying? If my mother was here, I wouldn't have the strength to ask. I needed to hold on to the belief that Nia would live.

"She's an amazing person."

"That she is."

"Zickar and his mate, Alwen, have been running your clan."

"My brother's the best. A mate, you say?" Even the thought of him finding someone to love couldn't drag my mind or gaze away from Nia.

Was she still breathing? I had to touch her to keep her with me.

"We'll talk in the morning," he said.

"Thank you, Turren."

He left, and I laid down on the furs beside Nia, carefully shifting until I could encircle her with my arms.

CHAPTER 33
NIA

I woke to warmth and someone kissing my temple.

"Nia. Love," Dakur whispered.

I opened my eyes, taking in the hide skin above me, the softness of what felt like furs below me. A glance to the right and through an opening showed the barest hint of the sun rising into the sky.

My chest hurt, but I was alive.

"I'm . . ." My voice croaked, and it even hurt to speak.

He rose on to his palm, looking down at me. So much sorrow shadowed his eyes. I couldn't drag my gaze from his. I belonged to this male. Completely.

"What happened?" I asked.

He shared that Blunt's arrow hit me in the chest and how a stone woman—stone woman? —named Pirrah had saved my life. How I'd been sleeping for two nights and one day. How he'd washed me, cared for me, and never left my side.

"Dakur," I said, sucking in just enough air to speak

but not enough to make my chest hurt any more than it already did. "I'm so sorry." I stroked his hair back across his shoulders, tracing my fingertip across the lines of worry on his face.

"Why are you sorry?"

"I fell asleep when I was supposed to watch. Brunt and his men found us. If I'd been awake, I could've . . ."

"What, run? He would've caught us. We had no way of escaping this, of escaping him. He would've followed us all the way to my forest. My only regret is that he hurt you."

A bolt of panic shot through me, and I tried to sit up, slumping quickly when pain overwhelmed me. "Where is he?"

"Dead. Taen ripped him apart."

"What a lovely shayde."

Dakur laughed, the sound half a groan. "He is at that. He's been pacing outside, worried about you, scaring the Ember orcs and Flazants out of their minds. They've heard of shaydes, and believe me, they have good reason to be scared, but you and I both know Taen wouldn't harm a chall."

Only Brunt, and I didn't feel any sadness about that. He'd been a horrible person all his life and this was the ending he brought to himself with his meanness.

"Can you take me outside so I can see the sunrise?" I asked.

Dakur's eyes widened. "Move you?"

"You said you . . ." Ugh. I didn't want to think about what he might've had to do while I was unconscious. I was sure I'd . . . *Yes, don't think about it.* "Anyway. I'd love to see the new day." The first of many for me and my love.

He carefully lifted me into his arms and carried me outside. Someone had placed a large rock near the front of the tent, and he settled on it. Around us, stone people were lighting a fire, and one was scooping up sand and actually eating it. Orcs strode about, some tending to . . . Yes, there were enormous birds here! I'd never seen anything like them before in my life.

Taen rushed over and licked my face, making me laugh. He flopped in the sand beside us, watching everyone intently.

An orc stopped in front of us, holding out a cake made of fruit and seeds, plus a flask that I prayed held water. "For you, Nia."

"I'm not sure . . ."

He bowed. "I'm Turren." His twinkling gaze met mine. "I'm caedos of the Ember Clan, and I hope before you leave to return to Dakur's home that you'll spend a little time with us. I plan to come to the next Mate Hunt, and I want to stop by and visit with you and Dakur on my way."

"You're welcome at my fire anytime," Dakur rumbled while I nibbled on the cake, washing it down with cool water from the flask.

Turren was as tall as Dakur and made up of a wall of rippling muscles. Other than his left arm covered with scars.

The wind caught his dark hair, sweeping it around

his face, and when he laughed, the world lightened as if it heard and couldn't do anything but agree with him that life was amazing.

I didn't know what the mate hunt was, but I wished him well with it. It was clear he'd helped me and Dakur, and that meant I'd welcome him whenever I saw him again.

He left me to finish eating, and Dakur's arms tightened around me.

"I thought I'd lose you," he rasped. "I didn't know what I could do to save you. I've never felt so helpless in my life."

I looked up at him, and he curled forward, kissing me.

Heat bloomed inside me, though I tamped it down. I wasn't well enough to be with him fully, but I suspected I would be soon.

"We have now," I said when he lifted his head. Snuggling deeper into his embrace, I watched as pink, gold, and orange bloomed across the sky like the prettiest bouquet ever. "It's a new day. A new beginning for us."

"I'll thank the fates every day of my life for giving me this second chance with you, love."

I took in the beauty of this world, of being with the male I'd always love.

We'd travel to his clan soon where I'd meet his family and see the wonders of his forest world.

Just as the colors etching across the sky announced a new day, reaching the forest would be the start of our wonderful life together.

CHAPTER 34
EPILOGUE
NIA

The Evening Before the Mate Hunt
Matis Clan

We'd invited all our friends to spend a fun evening before the Mate Hunt, and everyone was here.

Jaus and Rhoslyn had placed Shirra inside a fenced area to keep her contained. Their little girl was into everything. If they hadn't put her there with Eleri and Odik's daughter, the four adults wouldn't be able to sit and visit with us.

King Jaus and *Queen* Rhoslyn, that is. I still couldn't believe I was friends with the leaders of the orc kingdom. Not that they acted prissy or lifted their nose like I'd expect a king and queen to do. They behaved just like me and Dakur.

"So I told him that there was no way I'd pay him to transplant that many lindenmint bushes for such a high price," Rhoslyn said firmly.

Jaus grinned and patted her arm. They sat on a sofa we'd brought out from the central holding area along with other furniture for our guests, and his arm was around her shoulders. He was so much bigger than her, but that was also the norm when a human and orc mated.

He also adored her—it was clear in his eyes whenever he looked her way, which was often—another common occurrence when orcs and humans mated.

"Would the little ones like a ride?" Turren asked, his gaze locked on Shirra and Yusta.

"I imagine they would," Rhoslyn said with a laugh.

Eleri nodded and while Turren dropped to his hands and knees, she scooped up first her daughter, Yusta, and Shirra, placing them on his back.

Shirra clung to his horns, kicking his sides as he bellowed and crawled around on the platform.

"Shayde," Yusta shouted. "Fast, shayde!"

He kept moving around until he was clearly worn out. Still, his smile remained on his face. Finally, he sat and eased the little girls onto his lap, then started to tell them a story.

Since coming to this gorgeous forest home, my world had changed completely, solely due to Dakur and our love. We'd stayed with the Ember Clan until I was healed and then flew on voxes with Turren's clansmales all the way across the desert, a journey that only took a bit more than a day. They'd landed in a large meadow near where Dakur's clan made their home and boy, what a welcome we'd received.

I smiled at Dakur's mother, Tenkaril, who was gazing my way. She'd "seen" me a few times since we arrived here months ago, but she'd never revealed what she saw. She said it was only good, and that I'd savor it more if I let it unfold as the fates planned.

Did she know I was pregnant? I couldn't tell by the expression in her milky eyes, but I suspected she did. If she'd only seen good, she knew our child would be born easily, and that was enough for me.

Shirra and Yusta had fallen asleep. Rhoslyn gently took them and laid them on blankets inside the pen. They'd sleep for hours.

She returned, sitting with Jaus once more.

"You didn't finish the story," Eleri said to Rhoslyn. "What did he say when you told him you wouldn't pay that much? It's a lot of work transplanting lindenmint bushes, though well worth the effort since it keeps the dresalods from attacking and eating us." She suppressed a shudder. She and Odik, her caedos mate, lived on an island out in the sea, and Dakur and I had made plans to visit them soon. We should do so before our child was born, maybe in a few months. Their son sat on the sofa with them, listening raptly to the conversation. He was training with their teller of stories, and he was eager to absorb every word one of us spoke.

"He told me that was the price," Rhoslyn said with a sigh. "And I could either accept it or look elsewhere."

Jaus's grin widened. "My mate is feared throughout the kingdom for her thrifty ways."

"That's not true." She slapped his thigh and looked up at him. "They don't fear me."

"You don't deny you're thrifty." He leaned over to kiss her, his hand smoothing across her slightly rounded belly. She'd deliver a few months before me, and I hoped our orclings would be friends.

Zickar sat on yet another sofa with his mate, Alwen, his hand stroking her baby bump. She would deliver in six months or so, and she confided in me she hoped it was a girl.

They'd handled management of the clan so well while Dakur was away that the three of them had talked with the elders and divided the duties. For the first time, a clan had three caedos, and it was working out well already. Each had a knack for certain areas and since none of them were trying to handle everything at once, they could truly make their skills shine.

And now Dakur and I could take trips through the forest, wandering, so to speak, testing out tones with our pendants.

Dakur had suggested I, too, could join the caedos group, but my skill lay in healing, and I was soon working with the clan healers to learn everything I could from them while sharing what I'd learned while living in the desert village.

"Canape?" Alwen's mother, Roolina, asked, extending a wooden tray with snacks among us. She and her orc mate, Rusket, had taken over managing the kitchens, introducing human dishes everyone enjoyed while learning how to craft the most exquisite orc food. She loved living here and was very happy with Rusket, who adored her so much it made my heart hurt sometimes when I saw them together.

But then I'd see Dakur, and my heart would heal once more. He was everything to me, and I couldn't imagine living without him.

We ate snacks, washing them down with fillawate, which was made from a very rare fruit that grew deep beneath the ground. Because I was curious about stuff like that, I'd traveled with Dakur to pick it and helped make the brew. I loved how drinking it made me feel happy. We all needed to be cheered up every now and then.

A thump rang out behind us, and Dakur and I turned to find Mavileen and Pulost landing on the platform after being projected up from the ground by a teegar. I cupped my new pendant. Sessavia would soon teach me how to command teegars myself.

"There you all are." Mavileen strode forward, tugging Pulost along with her. She and other women had formed a new village on the edge of the forest, and Zickar and Alwen had convinced them it was worth being friendly with them rather than warring. Orcs from our clan and a few others now traveled here to visit the village, and many had formed mate bonds with the women living there. Pulost's clan pendant had flared the first time he met Mavileen, and while he'd had to convince her to mate with him, they were happy now and expecting their first orcling.

"Sorry we're late," Mavileen said, dropping down onto an empty sofa with Pulost. He put his arm around her and nodded to us all before his rapt gaze turned back to Mavileen. She was the true caedos of her village, and no one would take that from her, but Pulost stood by her side, supporting her at all times and contributing where he could, mostly when it came to the village's relationship with orcs.

I'd visited the village with Dakur and marveled at how efficiently the women ran it. Men should stop trying to suppress women all the time and let them shine. We made better partners than subordinates. Changing minds was an ongoing process, however, and I doubted I'd see the result I wished for in my lifetime. I'd be happy with small changes.

Madr and Lyneth arrived, Madr holding their young son. Lyneth was pregnant with their next orcling already, and her skin glowed. Her eyes as well whenever she gazed at Madr. I hadn't talked with either of them much, but we planned to stay with them in their mountain home when we took an extended visit to the city. We'd stay with Jaus and Rhoslyn a week, Madr and Lyneth another week, then finish our trip with a visit on the island with Eleri and Odik.

We'd recently received word from my village. With Brunt dead, everything had changed. I'd somehow inherited everything, a very strange concept to me. Since I didn't want to own, let alone run Brunt's businesses, I sold them to Kengart and Veegar.

They'd destroyed the arena and filled in the lower level of the compound. They were building a new one above ground, but instead of fights, they'd hold athletic competitions. Those who'd enjoyed betting on each battle could instead place money on who might throw a spear farther or who might lift more weight than any other. It sounded like a wonderful idea, and I was glad they'd thought of it. As for the other businesses, they'd run them well, treating everyone kindly.

People could change. Life could change. And this time, it was for the better.

As for the money, I didn't need it. With Jaus's help, we'd invested it in a new business in the city. If it did well, maybe one of our orclings would wish to run it. Otherwise, I'd hire managers and let the fates take the business where it needed to go.

Spying Turren standing against the rail a bit away from all of us, I rose.

"I'll be right back," I told Dakur.

He smiled and stroked my lower back as I passed him, returning to his conversation with the others.

I leaned against the rail beside Turren and stared out at the canopy. At night, it could be spooky and mysterious, but at any time of the day or night, it was still gorgeous. Small insects blinked their tiny lights on and off as they flitted about, and in the distance a shayde called. Taen and his siblings? They'd romped for hours after we arrived and had been inseparable since. They often slept in the home I now shared with Dakur, lounging on the wooden floor and gazing at us raptly as if they feared we'd disappear.

"It's a pretty night," I said.

"It is." Turren glanced at me before returning his gaze to the canopy. "I marvel at how different it is here when compared to the desert. Yet my heart still longs for the open sandy plains, the voxes we raise, and the migratory life my clan enjoys."

That was more words than I'd heard him piece together since he arrived. Silent and always watching, he rarely contributed to conversations. I sensed he might want to, but something was holding him back.

Turning, he leaned against the rail, facing me. He rubbed his scarred left arm, and I wanted to ask him what happened, but I sensed he'd close up and say nothing rather than share. "What do you believe will happen tomorrow during the hunt?"

"I want everything good and wonderful for you, Turren." He was a sweet, almost shy orc, and he deserved the best. Would he find someone who'd love him as much as I did Dakur?

Even now, my mate's gaze lingered on me with so much love, it made my skin tingle and my heart ache.

"To tomorrow, then." He saluted me with his glass of fillawate. His voice grew deep and raspy. "May my clan pendant glow for me."

"May it glow brightly," I said softly. Returning to sit with Dakur, I hoped for that with all my heart.

Tenkaril rose and with her assistant's help, she made

her way over to stand in the circle made by our many sofas. "I must go to bed." She stretched her back. "My bones are old. My mind is tired. But my heart and my special gift will remain on this world longer, the fate's willing."

Dakur got up and took her hands, looking down into her eyes that didn't see what we did of the world around us yet saw so much more behind the curtain. He kissed her cheek. "Rest well, Mother. I'll see you in the morning."

Stroking his cheek, she cackled. "I was correct, was I not, son?" Her gaze landed on Zickar. "As I was with you, to my other blessed son."

Zickar's arms tightened around Alwen holding their son on her lap. "Very much so."

Tenkaril looked back at Dakur. "I told you that you must go on a journey, that it would be fraught with danger."

Dakur held his hand out to me, and I joined him, him tucking me into his side.

Tenkaril nodded at me, though she kept speaking with Dakur. "I told you there was a chance you'd find your true mate and you have." Leaning over, she kissed my cheek. "You are a daughter of my heart just like Alwen. You have brought light and joy to our lives, and I adore you very much."

Tears pinched my eyes. "Thank you. You're wonderful." She'd taken the place of a mother in my heart, and I wanted to please her.

Tenkaril lifted her voice, and I knew she was

speaking to us all now, not just me and Dakur. "When I saw for my son before he began his treacherous journey, I told him that when he found his true mate," her hand squeezed mine, "things would get better for our clan. And look," her hand swept out to Shirra and Yusta sleeping in the fenced-in area, to Alwen and Zickar's son, Ferrin, plus all of us blooming with orclings who'd be born over the next year. "You have given our clans new life, new blood. And I only see wonderful things for us in the future. You've all made an old orc female happy."

Everyone got up and gathered around, each taking turns hugging her. We all adored her, and there wasn't a dry eye among us.

Tenkaril looked toward Turren who'd turned to lean his back against the rail, watching us together with a soft smile on his face. There was no mistaking the longing in his eyes as he took in every one of us, but now, I also saw hope.

"Tomorrow," Tenkaril told him. "Your pendant will blaze."

He sucked in a breath and straightened, his eyes pinning her in place. "You've seen this?"

"That, and so much more. Your mating, too, will change the future of the Ember Clan." She smacked her tusks and looked at all of us once more. "And I'm grateful that I'll be here to see it."

"I . . ." Turren looked ready to leap with joy. "Now I can't wait for the hunt."

With another cackle, Tenkaril left for her bed.

Everyone returned to the sofa to snack on Roolina and Rusket's treats and drink more fillawate.

After a bit, Dakur led me to a clear space at the rail and we stared at the stars winking through the canopy around us.

"Happy?" he asked softly.

"You know I am."

"My life could not be more complete, and it's because of you, my precious love."

He turned me in his arms and kissed me. My life had changed, and that was a true gift.

I couldn't wait to see what the fates had in store for us next.

I hope you enjoyed Dakur & Nia's story!
Next is Orc's Taming, and I bet you can't
wait for Turren's story!
Get Orc's Taming now!
Scroll forward for Chapter 1 . .

ORC'S TAMING

I want to begin a new life far from my village. Will that life include an orc who vows to adore me?

Kaila: When a man in my village makes demands I'm not willing to give into, my younger brother and I flee into the forest. It's the night of the Monster Mate Hunt, but the orcs who are gifted with brides in exchange for protecting the village will be too busy with the other woman to notice me.

Until Turren claims me as his mate. I'm not interested in marrying, and orcs scare me. But there's something sweet and endearing about this one. My brother and I planned to make a new life far from our village. Could that new life be with Turren?

Turren: Kaila's fierce and strong-willed, and in no time, I can't imagine a world without her. In exchange for taking her and her brother to the new village on the edge of the forest, she agrees to let me woo her during our journey. And me, a male of very few words, has talked her into giving me three kisses. I'm going to do all I can to convince her we're destined to be together, even if that means speaking of feelings and my past, things I've shared with no one.

When we reach the village, will Kaila leave me, or will she agree to be my mate?

Orc's Taming is Book 5 in the Monster Mate Hunt Series. Expect a seductive orc hero with a creative. . . (cough), size difference, a fierce, scarred woman who will do anything to protect those she loves, plus a fantasy world you'll want to live in. HEA guaranteed. Each book is standalone, but the series is more fun if read in order.

Monster Mate Hunt
Books in Order:

Orc's Mate
(a prequel novel –
FREE with newsletter sign-up)
Orc's Craving
Orc's Fate
Orc's Maiden
Orc's Captive
Orc's Taming

About the Author

Ava Ross is a two-time *USA Today* Bestselling author who has written numerous titles, all of them featuring sweet and steamy romance. She fell for men with unusual features when she first watched Star Wars, where alien creatures have gone mainstream. She lives in New England with her husband (who is sadly not an alien, though he is still cute in his own way), her kids, and a few assorted pets.

SERIES BY AVA

Mail-Order Brides of Crakair

Brides of Driegon

Fated Mates of the Ferlaern Warriors

Fated Mates of the Xilan Warriors

Holiday with a Cu'zod Warrior

Galaxy Games

Alien Warrior Abandoned

Beastly Alien Boss

Bride of the Fae

A Sci-Fi Holiday Tail

Monsterville, USA

Monster on Board

(co-written with Alana Khan)

Love at First Orc

Monster Mate Hunt

Brides of the Zuldrux Warriors

Monsters, PI

Single Titles

A Monster Worth Fighting For

Craving Stardust

Dad Bod Dragon

Mated to the Dragon

Jasmine's Grumpy Genie

Swamp Thing (You Make My Heart Sing)

You can find her books on Amazon.

CHAPTER 1
KAILA

"Your boss told me to come find you," my younger brother, Brunnen, said. "He said he wants to speak with you."

My sigh slipped out of me. I couldn't hold it back. Straightening from where I was weeding the village's vegetable garden, I turned to face Brunnen. I'd raised him since our parents died ten years ago when he was three and I was twelve, and there wasn't anyone I loved more than him.

I only kept this job because it came with a tiny house and my boss, Jabon, allowed Brunnen to stay there with me.

Sunlight highlighted Brunnen's black hair much like my own, and the sorrow in his green eyes we also shared hit me like a knife in the chest. He yanked on his shirt, and I pinched my eyes closed to shut out the sight of how the worn fabric outlined his thin frame. I worked incredibly hard, and I was allowed to take home the vegetables that had begun to spoil, but there was just never quite enough to sustain us both.

I was never enough.

"Did he say why he wants to talk with me?" I really didn't need to ask. He'd told me I must give him my answer by the end of today. *Answer?* He'd made a demand, and I told him I needed time to think about it. Because others were near enough to hear if I called out for help, he'd reluctantly agreed to my request.

Few would've rushed to my aid. We all needed our jobs, and Jabon could do what he pleased. Only Brunnen would've come over and socked Jabon. The last thing I wanted was for my young brother to attack my boss. He'd fire me, and we'd be homeless.

Slanting a quick look around, Brunnen lowered his voice. "We need to run, Kaila. I told you I've been saving. We can go to another village. I hear there's one on the other side of the forest run by women. If we ask the leader of that village nicely, she might let me live there with you. They'll take you in for sure. You're smart and plants sprout up just to stand in your light."

I stroked his cheek. "You're sweet to say that." A blush bloomed on his face, and he huffed, but I knew he still craved affection as much as me. "How much money do you have?" I was more curious than excited. A few pennies would not be enough to begin a new life.

I was beginning to resign myself to the fact that I'd have to tell Jabon yes.

Brunnen tugged some coins from his pocket and held

them out to me. So few. The color deepened in his face, telling me he was incredibly proud of what he'd collected.

"Where did you get them?" A thread of fear shot through me. Brunnen was sweet and innocent. It would be easy for someone to take advantage of him.

Stiffening his spine, he stood tall, towering over me, but I was tiny for a village woman. "I earned them. The smithy allows me to watch, and a few times, he's let me load wood into the burner or brace a particularly long piece of metal. He said if I'm diligent and fast, he might take me on as an apprentice soon."

"That would be wonderful." The apprenticeship would come with room and board.

He'd have no place with me if I agreed to Jabon's demands.

"Is this enough for us to run?" Hope clung to his words and in his eyes. I hated to crush his dream, but we'd need a lot more than that to outfit us for a long journey through the forest.

"Maybe." I nibbled on my lower lip. "I have a bit saved myself." Perhaps we *could* run. The Monster Mate Hunt would be held tonight, and in the furor, we might be able to slip from the fortress and race in the opposite direction. We'd find a place to hide until morning. After the orcs had claimed their brides, something they did annually in exchange for providing us protection from the shaydes, Brunnen and I could make our way through the woods to the village he'd mentioned.

I'd heard women had left other villages, tired of

being told what to do and given no freedom. They'd built a new home and ran things themselves, only taking husbands if they pleased.

No one made demands of them they weren't willing to fill. What would that be like?

"Kaila!"

Brunnen and I both jolted when Jabon bellowed my name.

I swallowed hard and tucked strands of my long hair behind my ear. They'd worked their way out of my braid. I was sweaty, sunburned, and dirt covered my clothing and face.

And yet, my boss would still want me.

"I'll go to him," I said softly. "I'll find a way to make him wait a little bit longer. That'll give us more time."

"I'm coming with you." My brother's lower lip trembled, but his eyes took on the flinty slant I remembered from our strong father who'd died trying to protect our mother, succumbing along with her. Brunnen might be slight and small for his age, but he was as fierce as me.

If he confronted my boss, he'd be in grave danger.

I gave Brunnen a pleasant smile, though I had to work hard to maintain it. "There's no need to come with me. Why don't you go home? Heat the soup I made for us last night. I'll be there soon, and we can eat it together." My belly rumbled at the thought of finally putting something in it other than water and a few raw vegetables.

Brunnen studied my face for a long while before jerking out a nod. "I don't like him. Not one bit."

It was funny how children could see right through a person to the evil festering inside.

I nudged his side. "Go. I won't be long."

After staring at me for a heartbeat, he turned and stomped down the row of beans and onto the main path winding through the big garden area. When he reached Jabon waiting, he paused, but after sending me a sad look, he continued past my boss and through the open gate beyond. Our small home was on the right, the last in a row of buildings offered to those who'd worked here the longest. I'd been employed in the fields for ten years.

I gathered my basket holding my water jug and the wrapper that had held the vegetables I'd eaten for lunch and walked toward Jabon. No one stood near him, unfortunately, so I wasn't sure I could use the pressure of others overhearing to get him to change his mind. He'd already given me an ultimatum, and I doubted I could stretch it much farther.

"It's time, Kaila," he said when I reached him, latching onto my upper arm. He pivoted and marched toward the central building where some ate their lunch, dragging me behind him. Everyone was either still working in the field or they'd left for the day. We rotated shifts to ensure someone was working in the gardens from before the sun rose until well past sunset. I'd worked the middle shift today.

Inside his office, he shut the door and pressed me against it, caging me with his palms on either side of my head.

I scooted beneath his arm and around his desk to put space between us. The open window behind could provide a route of escape, though there was no permanent way to avoid him forever, not if I wanted to hold on to this job.

"You agree?" he asked in a deadly voice.

"I need more time to decide."

He sighed. "There's no decision to make. You'll warm my bed, or you'll find another job."

"It's not fair. I'll tell the mayor."

"My brother?" He released a low laugh. "Do you truly think he'll protect you from me?"

"I pay taxes like everyone else." I stiffened my spine. "I'm entitled to have protection as much as the next person."

"You don't need protection from me."

Yes, I did. "Give me two more days, and I promise I'll . . ." I pinched my eyes closed, but I didn't keep them that way before snapping them open. No need to give him time to leap. "Then I'll come to your bed."

He grumbled but surely, he wanted me willing?

"Alright." He watched me, so I gave him a smile. "Two days, but no longer than that." His slick smile rose. "I'll be sure to change my sheets that day."

When he left, I wanted to collapse in his chair, but there was no way I'd remain in his territory. I scooted out the door, and spying him walking out into the field to speak with a different worker, I rushed to the right. I hurried home and shut the door, leaning against it while trying not to shriek.

"The soup's almost ready," Brunnen said, waving to the small table. He'd picked some wildflowers and propped the stems in a mug. "Sit. You worked hard today in the sun."

"You're the best person in the world." It was all I could do not to blubber. Tension spiraled inside me, but it was too late to think of any other way out of this but one.

"So are you, Kaila." He came over and hugged me, something he hadn't done for months, not since he turned thirteen. *I've grown up too much for that,* he'd said. *You understand.*

I did, but I missed being close to him. When he was little, he'd snuggle on my lap, falling asleep in my arms.

We sat and ate, and after, I leaned back in my chair, giving him a steady look. "I . . ." I hated to tear him from the only home he'd known, but we had no choice. My brother wouldn't survive here without me. And I couldn't bear the thought of lying beneath Jabon while he rutted.

"You're right," I said. "We need to run."

Brunnen nodded, his eyes widening.

"Let's combine our coins and go buy provisions." Rising, I took my bowl to the counter. Normally, I'd wash it in the central area. We had no running water in our home. After, I'd return it to the cupboard and tidy the small kitchen. We'd sit in the adjacent area, talking about general things or telling each other stories. Sometimes, we played a game we'd made up with sticks and smooth pebbles.

Not tonight.

"We'll pack our things," I said, turning to lean against the counter. "Tonight, we'll leave the village forever."

Get ORC'S TAMING Now

www.ingramcontent.com/pod-product-compliance
Lightning Source LLC
Chambersburg PA
CBHW031446160726
47994CB00005B/1897